An Augathella Easter

ANNIE SEATON

Augathella Short and Sweet: 6

This book is a work of fiction. Names, characters, places, magazine and incidents are the product of the author's imagination or are used fictitiously. Any resemblance to actual events, locales, or persons, living or dead, is coincidental.

Copyright © 2024 Annie Seaton

All rights reserved.

ISBN 978-1-923048-17-1

AUGATHELLA SHORT AND SWEETS

An Augathella Surprise

An Augathella Baby

An Augathella Spring

An Augathella Christmas

An Augathella Wedding

An Augathella Easter

An Augathella Masquerade Ball

Following on from:

THE AUGATHELLA GIRLS

Book 1: Outback Roads –The Nanny

Book 2: Outback Sky – The Pilot

Book 3: Outback Escape – The Sister

Book 4: Outback Winds – The Jillaroo

Book 5: Outback Dawn – The Visitor

Book 6: Outback Moonlight – The Rogue

Book 7: Outback Dust – The Drifter

Book 8: Outback Hope – The Farmer

CHAPTER 1

Spring - Eight months after Dr Harry and

Laura's wedding

The minute Bec Hunter met Chloe and Rosie, newcomers to town and proprietors of the New Life store and several other businesses, she knew instantly they were good people. It didn't take her long to get to know the girls; a couple of coffee dates at Jenna's Vintage Tea Room and one hilarious trivia night at the renovated pub with her partner, Matt and the girls' partners, Greg and Lex, saw a budding friendship firm up.

When the four new couples arrived in town back in March last year, Matt and Bec had been away. Bec was attending an intensive training course for her new job as a community youth worker at the Choice for Youth Centre in Charleville, and Matt had been catching up with some friends in Brisbane.

When they returned to Augathella after three months away, they were stunned by the changes that had taken place in town in that time.

Not only had they missed the arrival of the four new couples, the establishment of the new store, the pub renovations, and the new houses being built, but they'd also missed Harry and Laura's wedding.

'That'll teach us to stay put,' Matt said. He'd arrived in town with the nickname of the drifter, but since he and Bec had got together, Matt had taken to small-town life like a duck to water.

Bec grinned on the way home from Brisbane when he recounted the reaction of his city friends to the news that he had settled happily in the small town out west. 'They're running bets on how long I'll last,' he said, shaking his head. 'But I'm not going anywhere.'

'You'd better not be,' Bec said, squeezing his arm.

Life was good.

Bec and Matt had settled into a happy and contented relationship; he'd stayed at her house—and insisted on taking over the mortgage payments—and now she'd started her new job as a leader of the youth workers at the new community youth centre.

As the months passed and the four new couples settled into town, their friendship grew even more. They had a lot in common, and Matt loved playing with Travis, Chloe and Greg's little boy.

'I had the best night tonight,' Matt said as they walked home from the pub after collecting their prize for winning the trivia night. 'How amazing are those guys? So much energy.'

Bec slipped her arm through his.

'How amazing are you?' she said, leaning into Matt. 'You have an excellent knowledge of history. I thought you'd know all the song questions, but you blitzed the history ones too.'

'I was a model student at school,' Matt said, grinning down at her.

'That's not what you've told me before. Or what your mates said when they visited at Christmas.'

'Well, I enjoyed learning about the outback and the explorers. I fluked most of those answers tonight. But hey, I really enjoy spending time with those guys. They're fun. And Chloe has a wicked sense of humour.'

'She sure does.'

'I thought Gladys Tingle was going to come over and chip her for laughing so loudly. If looks could kill . . .'

'I saw that. Poor Gladys. She does like to be around everyone, but then she always looks so sour and disapproving.' Bec smiled up at Matt. 'You were kind to her tonight.'

'I think she's lonely. I did have a bit of a chat

with her. So did Chloe.'

'I didn't see that,' Bec said.

'You were talking to the Cartwrights. And how cute are those kids?'

Matt loved kids, no matter their age, but Bec had never had much to do with them. She had no family close by, and working in the aged care unit had made her wary of spending time with little ones. She had no idea what to do.

'Chloe's a good person. She brings happiness wherever she goes,' she agreed. 'I've had a lot to do with her and Rosie lately. Not so much with Leah and Gemma, but they seem nice too,' Bec said. 'The things they've done in town since they arrived here are almost unbelievable.'

'A breath of fresh air. And *young* fresh air,' Matt agreed. 'It's certainly given our town a lift.'

Our town.

Bec smiled. Matt had really settled into Augathella since he'd drifted in last year in his old van. And she had to admit that in the five years she'd lived here, she had settled too.

But he was right. The residents of the town had taken the enthusiasm of the new arrivals on board; houses were painted, extensions completed, gardens tidied up, and fences replaced. A new broom had certainly come to Augathella.

'And the population's growing too,' Matt continued. 'How cute is Chloe and Greg's little fella?'

Bec knew that Matt was looking at her, but she pretended to look at the seedlings that Gladys Tingle had planted along the footpath at the front of her house.

'Wow, look how many seedlings Gladys has planted out,' she said, pointing to the array of seedlings planted out in neat lines.

That was the one sticking point in their relationship, and it was the reason Bec kept saying no every time Matt mentioned marriage. He wanted kids soon; Bec wanted a career, and even though her new job was a total change of direction from nursing and studying for her Masters degree in dementia, she loved it. Working with young people—even though many were troubled—was refreshing.

'Hmm,' he said, putting his arm around her shoulder as they turned the corner to their house.

Bec took a deep breath; they'd had such a fun night, and she didn't want to get into a discussion now. When Matt had moved in with her while his arm healed after the accident when he'd saved Petie Cartwright at Sophie and Kent's wedding, Bec had no idea that he would end up moving in permanently. She'd had plans to finish her degree and move to Cairns, and then she'd gone and fallen in love with Matt Randall. She'd learned about his sad past, losing his girlfriend, Marianne, in a car accident that he'd been blamed for, and their love had grown.

And she loved him more every day; she just wasn't ready to have kids yet.

One day, she was sure she'd be ready.

Bec stopped at the fence on the far side of Gladys' property and looked up at Matt. His eyes were shadowed, and she knew she'd put the shadows there.

'I'm sorry, love. You know I'm not ready.' She tried to lighten her words. 'Anyway, with Laura and Harry's new little Henry and Chloe and Greg's Travis, there's no room for more babies in town. Not this year anyway.'

'You'd better tell Sophie and Kent that.' Matt smiled down at her, but she knew him well enough to know his smile was forced.

'Sophie's pregnant again?'

'Yes, Kent told me when I saw him at the pub the other night. I didn't tell you because I didn't want you to think I was pressuring you.'

Matt reached down and lifted a stray lock of hair from her cheek. 'And I'm not, love. I just wish you'd agree to marry me.'

'Maybe Gladys' garden isn't the right place to be having this conversation.' Bec reached up and kissed his cheek.

'Let's go home, and we'll talk about it,' Matt said hopefully.

CHAPTER 2

Bec – mid-summer

New gardens had been planted in every street in town, and blossoms began to appear on trees and shrubs.

January was quiet, with a few changes in town. The newcomers who had given a lift to an already lovely town relaxed and settled into their jobs.

Bec smiled as Matt backed the van out of the driveway one night in early February. At home, after the trivia night, Matt had agreed he was happy to wait until Bec had settled into her new career.

'Ask me at Easter,' she said. 'A proper proposal. And until then, just know how much I love you. Okay?'

'I can do that.' His smile was wide. 'I love

you too, Bec. And if you don't want to get married, that's okay.'

'Easter,' she said as he bent to kiss her.

Tonight, Matt was singing at the Tambo pub, and Chloe, Greg, Rosie, and Lex were travelling up in Matt's van with them. Ruth Mason had offered to mind Travis. There was plenty of room for all of them as well as Matt's sound gear.

'Thanks for taking us, mate,' Lex said as he climbed in after Rosie.

'You might as well have me as driver, and then if you want, you can have a drink or two.' One thing Matt never did was have even one beer when he was driving. Bec knew that he still carried emotional scars from the tragedy that had led to him leaving his life and career in Cairns four years ago.

Bec was pleased that Matt got along so well with their new friends. The guys had been off on a couple of camping weekends together—male bonding, Matt called it—and their social life had gotten even busier. Her new job took up a lot of her free time, but she loved what she did.

The evening was so still and warm that Matt had set up to play outside. The evening sky was a soft apricot, and a gentle breeze took away the lingering heat of the summer's day as they sat at the edge of the lawn in front of the outside bar.

The crowd was quickly building; Matt's reputation had spread. His gigs at small local pubs each weekend were attracting sizable crowds.

As he set up, the others chatted, and Bec's thoughts drifted to the issue that had been nagging at her for the last week. She sighed and looked over the paddock behind the pub.

'That was a big sigh. You sound like you've got the weight of the world on your shoulders. What's wrong?' Chloe asked as she passed over the wine that Greg had bought for Bec at the bar.

'Thanks. I'm just trying to nut out the Easter camp. We've got some funding, and I've got enough to hire two new youth workers, but that doesn't leave enough to run a camp for the ages I want to include.'

'There's a lot of interest already,' Chloe said as she sipped her soft drink. 'We were out at the Cartwrights last weekend, and Nigel and Rory were telling us about it. It's for all ages, is it?'

'We're hoping for ten and up. Since the national fitness camps have ended, there's nothing for the upper primary school kids. They have their end of Year Six school camp, but there's a need for more.' Bec held her hands up and shook her head at Chloe. 'And please don't think I'm asking you for money. I'll get a grant.'

'I wouldn't ever think that, sweetie. I simply asked why you sighed.' Chloe's eyes were wide and innocent.

Bec rolled her eyes when Rosie and Chloe

exchanged a significant glance.

'No, you're not giving me money for what I need. I'm in the middle of applying for funds and grants, and I'll get enough.'

'Tell us more about this Easter camp. Can we help? Can we come and volunteer? Can we cook or something?'

'Volunteers would be awesome,' Bec said. 'But you have to have your working with children checks and all the paperwork filled out, and I need to do risk assessments for all activities.'

'Sounds like you'll be busy,' Rosie said.

'I will be, but I love every minute of it,' Bec said with a smile.

'Where's it being held?'

'I think I've found a venue. It's far enough away from Augathella, so it will be new to the kids. There's this lake no one seems to have heard of. It's at the back of Quinn Calthorpe's property, about fifty ks out of town. We were visiting Quinn and Kimberley one weekend, and Matt decided to take a back road home.' Bec's voice filled with enthusiasm. 'You should see it. Two thick groves of trees that provide shade and a lake—not a dam—clear enough to swim in. There's even a sort of sandy beach on one side.'

'Who owns it? Quinn?'

'Yes, I rang him when I got home. It's on his property, and with the right paperwork filled out and approval of the relevant bodies, he's happy for the camp to be held there. I can get the buses to transport the kids up there without a problem. The council can get them as part of the contract with the local bus company, and I've had some good applicants for the youth worker position. It's mainly accommodation that's the problem. A lot of funding bodies aren't keen on providing grants for things that are ephemeral, like tents and barbecues and things like that. They want to see permanent structures before they approve the grants. Apparently, a lot of organisers keep the gear after it's purchased, and the benefactors are tightening up.'

Chloe and Rosie exchanged another glance. Bec shook her head. 'Like I said, don't even think about it, you pair.'

'Well, I'm not thinking about it for your camp specifically, but I think it would be a good idea for us to set up a retreat like that somewhere,' Chloe said. 'Then your community group and schools could use it for camps too.'

Bec sighed again. 'You guys are absolutely amazing. You have breathed so much life into our town and the district that you'll spread yourselves too thin. And Chloe, now that you've got Travis, you can't take on any more projects.'

Chloe grinned at her. 'Would you believe we're getting a bit bored? You know the department store is running really well. The

20

pub's really busy; we've just put on a third chef, and the butcher shop is gaining a really good reputation. We even had some customers come up from Charleville the other day.'

'It's all those gourmet cuts you've got in there. Matt reckons he's never eaten so well. So, Chloe, you all need to take a bow and have a break, not take on another project!'

They all turned as Matt's voice came over the microphone.

'I'm taking requests, ladies and gents. Hit me with your favourite songs.' He looked over at Bec and smiled. 'And I've got a special one to sing to my lady tonight.'

'Aw, Matt's so sweet,' Chloe said. 'Now let's enjoy the music. You can tell us more about your camp later on.'

Bec nodded, but her thoughts were still on her funding issue as Matt's voice filled the air.

CHAPTER 3

Jenna's Vintage Tearoom - Bec

Two weeks passed before the girls caught up again. On Saturday morning, they met for coffee at Jenna's tearoom.

Bec was running late. Matt had gone over to help Ben Riley build a shed at his parents' house, and Bec had started weeding the veggie patch. Time had gotten away from her as she mulled over funding grants while she trimmed the tomato bushes. Matt had a green thumb, and an excellent crop of tomatoes, lettuce, beetroot, and spring onions had complemented the meat from the new butcher shop each night.

She took a quick shower, pulled a clean dress over her head and slipped on a pair of sandals before jumping into her car and driving the short distance to the tearoom that her friend, Jenna, had established on the highway. Even though it was late summer, the car park already held several caravans and motorhomes. Jenna said the grey nomies were getting earlier each year.

As Bec hurried up the steps, Chloe and Rose waved to her from a table on the veranda.

'Hi, girls, sorry I'm a bit late. I was weeding Matt's garden and lost track of the time.'

'No problem. We thought you might have been working,' Rosie said. 'We were just about to order.' She waved to Jenna, who immediately came over to the table with an order pad.

'Good morning, girls. Good to see you all out and about on this lovely Saturday morning,' she said.

'Hi, Jenna, how are you?' Bec said.

'Absolutely flat chat,' Jenna said. 'We've been so busy. We did so many hot breakfasts this morning poor Ellie is just about run off her feet. What can I get you today?'

'The usual coffees, please,' the three girls replied.

'And may I tempt you with Ellie's new specialty?'

'I saw some interesting cakes in the cabinet as we walked in,' Chloe said. 'What's the specialty today?'

'Tiramisu slice.'

'Yum, yes, please.'

Jenna quickly wrote the orders and walked away.

'Where's Travis?' Bec asked as she looked around for the pram that Chloe seemed to have with her all the time.

'I asked Greg to mind him because we wanted to have a chat with you.'

Bec frowned. 'A chat with me? Sounds like I'm in trouble.'

Chloe chuckled. 'No, of course not. I wanted to talk to you about your Easter camp. I loved going to camps when I was a kid *and* into my teens. I have fond memories of romance back in those days.'

'Romance? What sort of camp was it?' Bec asked. 'One of those fitness camp ones that we went to at high school?'

'No, it was a youth camp. I had a friend whose dad was a minister, and she used to drag me along there to Sunday school sometimes. I found that a bit boring as I got into my teens, but I loved the youth fellowship on Friday nights. We used to go sand surfing on the dunes at the back of Anna Bay sometimes. We had so much fun.'

'Anna Bay? Where's that?' Bec asked.

'North of Newcastle, before you get to Port Stephens. I spent some of my childhood in Newcastle, and I learned a lot about the region and various sites on those Friday nights. I made new friends and that year we went off to a couple of camps.' Chloe chuckled. 'I saw a different side to some of those kids. They ran wild while the poor youth workers were running around all night with torches trying to find them all around the side of the lake.'

'Don't tell me that. I'll have to add torches to my list for our camp,' Bec said.

'I was fifteen.' Chloe's cheeks went pink with a pretty blush. 'The camp was at Lake Macquarie and that's where I had my first kiss. I always thought of it when Mum and Dad drove past it up the motorway before we moved to Brisbane. I learned a lot about the area when we lived down there. We went to lots of different places every Friday night.'

'Sounds like a lot of fun. That's what I want to make our camp for the local kids. Fun that leaves lifelong memories.' Bec turned to Rosie. 'Where did you have your first kiss?'

Rose giggled. 'Makes me sound like a bit of

a tart. Would you believe in the back seat of the bus on the way home from school?'

Bec laughed. 'How old were you?'

'I was only fourteen,' Rosie admitted. 'Now, Bec. Your turn. What about you?'

'Well, it's pretty embarrassing after listening to you, but at fourteen and fifteen, my life was pretty sheltered.'

'Come on, tell us. First kiss. How old were you?'

'Would you believe seventeen and a half, my last year of high school? At the year twelve farewell.'

'Was he your boyfriend?'

'He was, and he was a lovely guy. We actually did go out on a few dates for a couple of months until I headed off to uni to do my nursing, and then he headed off somewhere. We lost touch. But those memories are sweet.'

'It was a special time, wasn't it?'

'It was. So what have you girls been up to the last couple of weeks while I've been ploughing through grant applications?' Bec asked.

Chloe and Rosie exchanged a glance. 'Well, as much as it's been nice sharing memories, we do actually have an ulterior motive. We wanted to speak to you, Bec.'

'Okay, what about?'

'Well, we went for a drive last weekend, and we just happened to stumble upon your lake.'

'Oh?' Bec said suspiciously. 'You just happened to stumble upon *my* lake? I don't own a lake.'

'Quinn's lake.'

'That's a long way to go for a drive.'

Chloe's eyes were wide with innocence. 'It was. And we just happened to bump into Quinn and Kimberley while we were out there.'

'Wow,' said Bec. 'They just happened to be

down at the back of their property on the lake. Come clean, you guys. What were you doing out there?'

Chloe's smile was wide and still innocent. 'Well, we knew that you were after the grants, and we know that you're having problems because it was tent accommodation and not permanent dwellings, so we got to thinking.'

'Okay, tell me about thinking.' Bec narrowed her eyes.

'Quinn and the rest of us have come to an agreement.' Rosie said with a nod.

'We've bought some land off him,' Chloe added.

'You've bought some land?' Bec widened her eyes. 'Just like that?'

'Don't be cross. It's not just because you're having a camp. We're not stepping on your toes, Bec.' Rosie looked worried.

'I'm not cross. I am filled with awe at what

you guys can achieve with very little effort.'

'It's sad that it boils down to money,' Chloe said. 'But being in the position that we're in since we had that win means we can create change more quickly. We can see where it's needed, and we can try to contribute.'

Bec shook her head. 'You guys deserve an award. Citizens of the century. The difference you have made to this town has been amazing. And not just cosmetic changes; you've made a difference to many lives already.'

Chloe's smile was gentle. 'You know the most wonderful thing about our situation? If we get an idea, we don't have to worry about how we can implement it. We can just go ahead and do it. We've been blessed, and it is up to us to share our good fortune and make a difference where we can.'

'Tell me more,' Bec said.

'We thought about it the weekend after Matt

sang up at Tambo,' Chloe said. 'There was an obvious need for a venue for all sorts of things.'

Rosie interrupted. 'Like yoga retreats, women's weekends, men's camps, all sorts of things that can contribute to the mental health of our community. And you're doing the same in your job with the youth in the district, so if—'

Bec leaned back and folded her arms. 'Hang on, here comes Jenna with our coffee.'

Jenna placed three cups of coffee on the table. 'I'll be back with your slices shortly,' she said.

'Okay, Chloe, keep going,' Bec said once Jenna had gone back to the kitchen.

'Quinn sold us just a little strip of land along one side of the lake. We didn't want to interfere with his property, and we didn't want to take his lake away from him, but he was more than happy to sell us that strip of land.'

'He's also agreed to put in a new road from

the highway, but it will be gated, so not just anyone can drive out to the lake. He's happy for us to build some permanent structures there too,' Rosie added.

Bec kept her arms folded and shook her head as Chloe and Rosie picked up their cups and sipped their coffee. 'Really,' she said slowly. 'You've achieved that much in only two weeks?'

'What it means now is that you can concentrate on your funding grants for staff and food and stuff like that, but if you want, we'd love you to have your Easter camp on the land we've bought from Quinn.'

'I'd love to, but our camp's only eight weeks away. It won't be ready in time.' Bec reached for her coffee as Jenna appeared with their food. 'Yum, that looks divine.'

Chloe reached out and put her hand on Bec's arm. 'No, it will be ready. Our builder, who did the renovations for the pub, was happy to slip the building of the cabins in between other commitments. Ben helped us fast-track the plans through council, and as a favour, Greg and Lex are helping him do some work at his parents' house this morning.'

'Matt's there too,' Bec said. 'What about Travis? I thought Greg was minding him.'

'Jenny said she'd keep an eye out when he had a sleep, and I'm picking him up after we're done here.'

'You girls have got it all organised, haven't you?' Bec said. She'd always been a bit of a loner, but Chloe and Rosie had become close friends over the past months. But what they had done now filled her with appreciation for what special people they were. She blinked back tears.

'I hope you don't mind, Bec. It's not like we've taken over your initiative. If you still want to get tents and swags and things like that for a real camp, we'll just keep building our retreat on the other side of the lake. We don't expect you to come if you'd prefer the other way.'

'No, of course not. We'll be there with bells on. I think you're absolutely wonderful. It means now that I can advertise for the youth workers. Now that I don't have to worry about tents and swags and figure out how to overcome that hurdle, I can definitely hire two, maybe three. If we have three, we can have the two age groups there. So, tell me about these buildings that are getting built.'

Chloe was full of enthusiasm as she described their plans, and Bec's thoughts churned wildly as she heard her describe four separate dormitories, two ablution blocks, a cookhouse, and a big open-air fire pit for the winter camps.

Bec's hand shook as she held her cup. She put her cup in the saucer and lifted her hand to wipe the tears from her eyes.

Chloe looked at her and shook her head. 'Don't go crying, Bec. What's the matter?'

'Do you know how many people would've won a fortune like you guys? Would've bought flash houses for themselves and fancy boats and overseas trips, or wasted it? You guys are making a difference. And you keep it so quiet. It's an absolute credit to you, what you're doing. I'm simply overwhelmed,' Bec said. 'Thank you so much.'

Chloe and Rosie both looked embarrassed. 'We love doing what we're doing.'

CHAPTER 4

Bec - February

Bec stood at the door of the CFY office at the back of the Charleville shire chambers. Rivers of water covered the green grass in the flat back area, and the barbeque table, where they often sat and had meetings or morning tea and lunch, was almost underwater in the far corner.

She turned to Alice, her offsider. 'It doesn't bode well for our Easter camp, does it, Alice?'

'It will be fine. I think this is just localised rain. I had a look at the BOM site before, and we're copping it about ten kilometres around Charleville. I reckon you'll go home tonight, and Augathella will still be as dry as a bone. And remember, the lake is another fifty ks northwest from there too. I'm sure it'll be fine. And if it is raining a bit there, it'll mean more water in the lake. And green grass.'

'I love your confidence. Well, I'm going to cross my fingers and toes, and I'll be looking at that weather site for the next four weeks.'

'It's only a localised storm, late summer rain,' Alice said.

'I don't know, my first year at Augathella, they kept saying it was going to be dry, and we had the wettest winter on record. We've put so much work into organising this camp and getting the funding for it. I'll be so disappointed if it has to be cancelled due to the weather.'

Alice, ever the optimist, shook her head. 'Bec, if it's cancelled—and it won't be—we'll reschedule. We'll have some disappointed kids, and it won't be an Easter camp. We won't be having the Easter activities, but we can do other things at another time. Maybe the next school holidays long weekend.'

'I guess you're right.' Bec stared at the fat raindrops still splashing in the puddles. 'Matt says I'm a worrier. He's always telling me to chill.' She chuckled. 'I just don't want to chill as much as he does.'

'Has he been enjoying working as an accountant again?'

'He has, but between you and me, I think he enjoys his singing nights more.'

They both turned and headed back inside, closing the door behind them.

'I've been going through the applications for the youth workers.'

'Got many good ones?'

'Yes, interviews are on Friday. I think it's going to be hard to choose. I'm going to read through them all again tonight.'

'Many applications?'

'Twelve. I'll hand them over to you when I finish.' Alice was on the panel as well.

'Don't you work too hard.'

'It's fine. I work at home when Matt works.

The word is spreading about how good he is, and he's picked up a heap of new clients, not only in Augathella but also in Charleville and Tambo. He doesn't know if he's Arthur or Martha at the moment. I think he spends more time on the road than I do. It's not at all what he imagined when he set up his home office. I think he had visions of working a few hours a day at home, and that was it.'

'But is he enjoying it?'

'He loves it. He whinges, but I can tell he enjoys what he's doing. He's making a difference.'

'What about his singing? He's fabulous,' Alice said. 'We heard him at the club on Saturday.'

'Well, he's got a regular gig at the Tambo pub, and he's had a few offers from Blackall, but he's saying no for the time being. It's a bit far to drive home after a show.'

Alice's look was coy. 'And you two still getting on as well as you always did?'

'Of course, we are,' Bec said. 'I adore the man.'

Alice pulled a mock face. 'Well, a girl can only hope. I grew up in Augathella, and all the good catches left town after high school. That's why I moved to Charleville. I think I'm destined to never find love.' Alice put a hand on her chest and sighed. 'Hire a good-looking youth worker around twenty-five. That would suit me.'

Bec smiled. 'You'll meet someone one day. Matt was the last person I imagined would come into my life.'

'But he worked hard at it, didn't he?'

'He surely did, but I knew pretty much from the beginning that he was the one.'

'You dark horse, you never let on.'

'I was too busy then, working at the hospital. By the time Matt and I got together, I was pretty much burned out.'

'And you've got no regrets doing youth work now?' Alice asked.

'I said I'd give it a try and see how I went. I only took leave from the hospital, but I've loved every minute of it. I actually put in my notice at the hospital a couple of weeks ago, so I hope the funding stays up for our centre.'

'I'd love to know who funded it,' Alice said. 'Apparently, it's hush-hush, and no one is letting on where it came from. That worries me a bit in case it does go.'

'It's certainly been generous. I mean, look at the new office.' Bec changed the subject as she gestured around to the freshly painted walls, the brand-new furniture and the two new computers. Even the little kitchenette had been refurbished with a new benchtop. It had previously been a room that the museum had used to store things, and now it was a lovely workplace.

When it wasn't raining, that was.

She had her suspicions as to the funding source, but Chloe and Rosie had never said anything, and it wasn't her place to ask. She knew that they had built the retreat as the venue for the camp, and that was all she needed to know.

'Okay, I've got a couple more submissions to do,' Bec said, 'and then I'm going to call it a day and drive home. I hope it's not raining all the way to Augathella.'

'Which road do you take?' Alice asked.

'I think I'll go the main highway today; there's more chance of water not lying there than there is on the back one. There are a few hollows along that way; I'd hate to get stranded.'

'I'm going to leave now. I'm going to visit my gran.'

'How's she going?'

'Well, it took six months to persuade her to

go into the aged care facility, but you know what? She's loving every minute. The day she arrived, the residents had made a huge fresh floral bouquet to welcome her, and she hasn't had one regret since she arrived. I've never seen her so happy. She's joined every club that's going and watched more movies than she ever watched at home, and she's put on about three kilograms, so that proves to us that she wasn't eating properly when she was looking after herself.'

'And you're still living in her house?' Bec asked.

'Yeah, Gran doesn't want to sell it, so while she was able to afford the fees for the aged care facility, I still insist on paying rent, and she reckons she's just putting it away for me to get when she carks it! Her words!'

'I love your grandmother,' Bec said. 'I met her a couple of times when I used to come down to the hospital from Augathella when she was in with her broken hip.'

'She's a sweet thing, isn't she?' Alice said.

Bec reached over and hugged Alice. 'Just like her granddaughter. I love working with you too, Alice. Okay, I'm going to hit the road; I'll see you later.'

'Remember, Bec?' Alice called after her as Bec reached the door.

She turned with a frown. 'Remember what?

'Twenty-five and good-looking.'

Bec was still smiling when she got in her car.

CHAPTER 5

Bec's smile was still there as she turned off the highway. For a moment, she had considered pulling up at Jenna's tearoom, but she thought Jenna had probably turned off the machine for the day. Besides, she had a perfectly good coffee machine at home; she could make a coffee there when she arrived home.

Alice had been right; the rain stopped exactly ten kilometres north of Charleville, and Bec had driven into afternoon sunshine. The weather out west never ceased to amaze her, and it was hard to predict what it was going to do. Everyone thought it was dry and hot out here all the time, but she'd been pleasantly surprised in the years since she'd moved to the district. It was a beautiful climate, and the countryside was as pretty as anything she'd seen on the coast.

Matt's car wasn't in the driveway, and she pulled a face. She had been hoping to sit and relax and have a coffee with him. She picked up her briefcase, locked her car, and climbed up the front steps. Putting a key in the lock, she called out anyway, just in case he was parked around the back. 'You home, Matt?'

She was met by silence, and when she got into the kitchen, there was a handwritten note on the kitchen bench: 'Hi sweets, I had to go out to Braden's place, so I'll probably be late. I made a booking at the pub. I'll meet you there for dinner at seven.'

'Oh, good.' Since the newcomers had refurbished the pub and taken it over, it had been an extremely popular place in town. Not that it hadn't been before, but these days it was essential to book, no matter which night of the week you went for dinner. Sean had taken over the management of the whole business and was still cooking occasionally when needed, but there was a new chef from the Sunshine Coast, and the pub was starting to get excellent reviews in the city. Sean said he preferred being out in the bar to keep up with the locals.

Bec had noticed the few times they'd been there and sometimes on the weekend when they drove past that there were some luxurious cars and sports cars parked there on a Saturday night.

The rooms upstairs had also been refurbished, and the Augathella pub was now rated a five-star establishment.

She took a quick shower and went to the wardrobe, looking for something pretty to wear out. If the pub had been done up, she could make an effort too. She knew Matt would be late. She grinned. He always was, so there was no rush to get ready.

Maybe she could make a couple of referee calls.

Kimberley Calthorpe had been named as a referee on two of the applications, and Bec guessed that the applicants were either locals or had been at some point.

As she dried her hair and pulled it up into a clip, the early evening was still warm, even though Easter was approaching quickly. She thought about the benefactor who supported everything they were doing for the district's youth. The only prerequisite for the funding was that they use the name "Choice for Youth," and Alice, Bec and the members of the shire council who accepted the funding were certainly happy to go along with that.

Bec had been writing submissions for government grants and funding towards other initiatives. Even though the funding was good and they now had a venue for the camp, she still had some other ideas that would need funding. If there's one thing Bec had, it was grand plans and big ideas because she thought if no one had them and no one tried for them, it would never happen.

Ideas were forming as she sat down at her laptop and pulled up the applications on the screen.

She had chosen five to interview. one females and four males had fulfilled all the criteria and had listed referees.

She scanned through the applications of those she had chosen to interview and who had been approved by the human resources officer at the council: Matilda Tingle, a part-time youth worker from Brisbane—Bec had wondered if she was related to Gladys. Tingle was an unusual name. Jeremy Johnson, currently working as a nurse in St George; Rory McArthur, a mine worker; Brian Harris, a children's librarian at Charleville; and Neil Evans, who had listed himself as currently a full-time father but had extensive experience in the youth work sector.

Bec glanced at her watch; it was six forty-five. If she left for the pub a bit after seven, she could guarantee she'd still beat Matt. She'd call Kimberley and ask her for a reference for the two who had listed her as their first referee: Matilda Tingle and Jeremy Johnson.

Kimberley would be home from school by now, and Bec hoped she didn't interrupt their dinner. She dialled the number and waited, but the call eventually went to voicemail.

'Hello, you've reached Kimberley Calthorpe. Please leave a message, and I'll get back to you.'

'Bec Hunter, Kimberley. No need to call back, I'm going out, so I'll catch you tomorrow.'

With a last swipe of lipstick over her mouth, Bec picked up her purse and keys, and locked the front door behind her. The twilight bathed their small house in soft light, and she smiled as she noticed Matt had mowed the footpath and weeded the front gardens, in between the many jobs that she knew he had on today. He must have had a call from Braden Cartwright, as he hadn't mentioned going out there when they'd had breakfast together this morning.

Every morning, Matt listed for her what jobs he had on that day. She suspected he was trying to justify working from home, so she broached the subject one morning last week.

'Sweetie, you don't have to tell me what you're doing. I know you work hard, and even if you just wanted to sing at the pubs, I'd be happy with whatever you chose to do.'

Matt walked over when she picked up her keys, put his arms around her, and kissed her cheek. 'Do you know how much I love you, Bec Hunter?'

'As much as I love you, I hope,' she said. His lips moved to hers, and Bec was quite late for work that morning.

So he'd mowed the lawn, weeded the gardens, and headed out to Braden's today. Sometimes, she wondered if he spent so much time out there because he enjoyed playing with the kids. He and Petie had a special bond from the night that Matt had saved him from more serious injury at Sophie and Kent's wedding, and they got on like a house on fire.

She also noticed when he was nursing Braden and Callie's twins, Meggie and Munro, how much he enjoyed playing with the babies now. They were sitting up and taking notice and babbling back to him. One day he would make a great father.

One day, when she was ready.

Guilt trickled through Bec. Maybe she needed to look at her priorities.

She wasn't quite ready yet, but she would like to have children before she was thirty, but that was a couple of years away. She just hoped that Matt could wait and it didn't cause any friction between them.

CHAPTER 6

The Cartwrights and the Rileys

'Are you nearly ready, Brae?' Callie called out as the six o'clock news blared from the television in the kitchen where Meggie and Munro were sitting in their high chairs having dinner. 'We can't be late; Matt was most particular that we had to be there before seven o'clock. That's the time he told Bec to be there.'

'Yeah, darling, thank you. Don't get your knickers in a twist. I've just got to find a clean shirt,' he called from up the hall.

'Braden Cartwright, there are plenty of clean shirts hanging up in our wardrobe.'

He came into the kitchen with a wide grin, dressed in his good trousers and favourite shirt, with his damp hair slicked back. 'Yep, I was just winding you up.'

Callie pulled a face at him. 'What about the

boys?'

'Dressed, clean faces and boots on, watching TV in the family room.'

'Right,' she said. 'You finish feeding this pair and make sure you keep them clean while I go and get changed. I had my shower when they were napping. When they're done, just wipe their faces and hands. They're ready to go into the car seats.'

'You're an amazing woman, Callie,' he said, dropping a kiss on her cheek.

'I am. I'm clever. I married you. Come on, Braden, we have to be on time.'

***

Jenny Riley stood at the doorway of the living room and frowned at her husband, Tom. 'Are you ready to go yet?'

'Go? Go where?' he asked as he picked up the remote and turned the news down. 'Where are we going?'

55

'I told you this afternoon we were going to Bec Hunter's surprise birthday party at the pub. Matt booked the whole dining room out about three months ago.'

'You didn't tell me.' Tom threw the remote into the basket and stood there looking at her.

'Yes, we talked about it this afternoon, sweetheart.' A trickle of worry went through Jenny. 'Don't you remember us talking about it over a coffee?'

Tom looked at her and shook his head. 'I'm sure we didn't.'

Jenny frowned. It was about the third time in the last couple of weeks that Tom had been forgetful, and she was getting a little bit concerned. It was time for him to see Dr. Harry and have a check-up. He was almost seventy, and she was worried. Hopefully, it was just his usual vagueness.

'Go and have a quick shower, and I'll put

some clothes out on the bed for you. Ben and Amelia are picking us up in about fifteen minutes.'

'I'm coming, I'm coming,' he said. 'Can I just watch this item?'

'No, Tom, go and get ready now.'

'Yes, dear.' He threw her a grin and disappeared down the hall; maybe it was just his usual absentmindedness that had kicked in this afternoon. She really hoped it was since she wasn't going to say anything to Ben because she didn't want to worry him.

'Hi, sweetheart,' she said five minutes later as Ben stepped through the front door.

'Where's Amelia?'

'They're waiting in the car; we thought we'd drive you and Dad down to the pub a bit early. If you're ready . . .'

'I'm ready, but your father forgot we were going.'

Ben looked concerned, and Jenny looked at her son, wondering why he was frowning. 'What's wrong, love?'

'Mum, have you noticed anything a bit strange with Dad lately?'

An ice-cold knife seemed to plunge into Jenny's chest. She put her hand there and rubbed. 'Why, what's wrong? Why do you ask, Ben?'

'I don't want to worry you, but just a couple of times in the last month or so, Dad's totally forgotten things I've already told him. And he asked me one day last week when the NRL grand final was.'

Jenny sighed. 'Would you believe I was just thinking the same thing, and I decided not to mention it to you? I didn't want to worry you.'

'Perhaps a visit to Harry?' Ben suggested.

'I think so, but trying to get your father to go to the doctor is like trying to pull teeth,' she said.

'Do you want me to talk to him about it, or

do you want me to come over, and we'll both talk to him together?'

'No, I think if both of us talk to him and make it into a really big deal he'll be a bit upset, and feel that we've been talking about him behind his back. Leave it with me, Ben, I'll sort it.'

'Sort what?'

They both jumped and turned around as Tom walked into the living room.

'Didn't you have a shower?' Jenny said.

'Just a spray of deodorant.' Tom grinned. 'I heard Ben arrive, so I thought I'd be quick.'

'What about the shirt I put out for you?'

'What shirt?' Tom said, looking down 'Nothing wrong with this one. It's comfortable.'

Jenny reached out and took his hand. 'Okay, you look fine.'

'Gidday, son.' Tom went over and hugged Ben. 'Good to see you. It's been a while.'

Ben's eyes widened as he held Jenny's gaze for a few seconds. 'Yeah,' he said.

Jenny pushed away the worry that gripped her. Ben had been over for dinner last night with Sebastian while Amelia went to a planning meeting for the ball they were organising later in the year.

***

Bec

Bec chose to walk down to the pub because it was such a lovely evening. It was hard to believe that so much water had been running in the yard at Charleville, and here, it was dry as Alice said it would be.

Alice had grown up in the district, and Bec appreciated her passion for doing the right thing for the district's youth. However, Alice had much more local knowledge, and when Bec applied for grants and funding, Alice suggested different places that she could use as examples and different funding sources. Alice Templeton was a mine of information.

As Bec crossed the road, turned onto Main Street, and approached the pub, she smiled as Sophie and Kent Mason got out of their four-wheel-drive. Her smile widened as Fallon and Jon parked behind them and lifted out little Ryan, who was now toddling around.

'Hey, guys, are you having dinner here tonight?' she said.

'Hi Bec,' Sophie said, reaching over and kissing her cheek. 'I haven't seen you for ages.'

'Now that I'm working down in Charleville, I don't see people nearly as much,' she said.

'How's the new job going?' Fallon asked.

'I love it,' Bec said.

'You look a lot more relaxed. I suppose it's the pretty dress, not in the hospital uniform, that makes you look different.'

'And no stress,' Fallon said. 'You look lovely, Bec.'

'Thank you.' Heat ran up her neck; she hated people commenting on her appearance. Bec had always felt as though she didn't have much fashion sense, and most of the time, it didn't bother her. 'I figured I'd better get dressed up. It's pretty swish in there now. Are you guys staying for dinner?'

'Yeah, we are. Have you guys booked?' Sophie glanced at Fallon.

'Yes, we have.'

'I'm not sure whether Matt's booked just for the two of us or not. I don't know what else he's planned.'

Sophie and Fallon exchanged another glance, and Bec was disappointed when they didn't suggest that perhaps she and Matt could join them anyway. They probably wanted to have a chat together; Sophie and Fallon were friends.

'Okay, we might see you in there. I'm going to go to the front bar and get a drink while I wait for Matt,' she said.

***

'You were running late too?' Sophie asked Fallon quietly as Bec went through the side entrance of the pub.

'Yes, Ruby was fussing,' Sophie said. 'How mean did I feel not asking Bec to join us?'

'Matt is a great guy, but I don't think he thought this through very well.'

'When's Bec's birthday? Do you think she suspects?'

'I don't think she's got any idea at all. Her birthday is next Saturday, but Matt said he was singing up at Tambo, and he felt bad that he hadn't realised the date before he accepted the gig. That's why he's organised the surprise party for tonight.'

63

'Well, Bec's certainly going to get a surprise. I'm so pleased she got dressed up. She would've killed him if she'd turned up in jeans and a T-shirt.'

'She looked lovely, didn't she?'

'She did. She's obviously loving her new job.'

'From what I've read in the paper, they're doing a great job. Alice Templeton is a lovely girl too.'

'The youth of Charleville and Augie are very lucky, and from what I hear, Tambo and Cunnamulla too,' Fallon added.

'It's certainly made a difference to our district.'

'Not to mention what our new friends in town are doing. Did you hear that they're building a retreat out near Quinn Calthorpe's place now?' Fallon handed Ryan over to Jon as he stood beside Kent, who was nursing Ruby

Rose.

Sophie and Fallon chatted as they walked in together, behind Jon and Kent, and chose a table close to the entrance.

'Easier to get out in the event of a crying baby,' Fallon said.

Sophie grinned. 'I hear you.'

CHAPTER 7

Kimberley

'Excuse me for a moment, Callie. I need to take this call. I think it's Lindy. I probably need to find a substitute for her class for next week.'

Callie smiled and took Megan back from Kimberley as she reached for her phone on the table.

'I'll be back in a moment,' she said to Quinn on her way out to the side entrance. As soon as she was through the door, she pressed the answer icon. 'Kimberley Calthorpe.'

As she put the phone on speaker, Kimberley glanced at the number. It wasn't the one she'd been expecting. Lindy's husband had been ill for a couple of weeks, and they were going to Brisbane for him to have some tests. She'd expected that call, but it looked like it was someone else calling.

Please, no one else be sick for school next week. Substitute teachers were short.

'Hello, Kimberley,' said an unfamiliar voice. 'I don't know whether you remember me or not. It's Matilda Tingle. You might remember me as Tilly.'

'Tilly, of course I do,' Kimberley said. 'How are you? I haven't seen you for years.'

'It's been a long time. I haven't been back to Augathella since I left high school,' Tilly replied.

'Well, it's good to hear from you now. What can I do for you?'

Kimberley and Tilly had been great mates for the last two years of high school, but as always happens when everyone finishes that final year, they'd headed off in different directions. Kimberley had headed off to Brisbane to do her teaching degree, and she wasn't sure where Matilda had gone.

The phone was silent. 'It's so good to hear from you,' Kimberley repeated.

'Sorry, I was just distracted here. I'm waiting for a ferry, but it was the wrong one.'

'Ferry? Where are you?'

'I'm in Brisbane. I've got a big favour to ask, Kimberley. I know you haven't seen me for ages, but I was hoping that someone from Augathella might be able to help me a little bit.'

'Why's that? What's happened?'

'Well, I'd like to come back to town. My grandma's getting on, and I suspect she needs me. I don't know if you remember Gladys Tingle or not.'

Kimberley smiled. 'Not only do I remember her, we're at the pub for a birthday party tonight, and your grandmother is here too.'

'Oh, that's good to hear. How does she look?' Tilly asked.

Kimberley answered carefully because

Gladys wasn't a popular person in town at the best of times. Every town had a busybody, and Gladys was Augathella's finest. The sad part was she was often negative.

'She looks fine. Actually, very well. We've had a lot of new people in town who've started new businesses, built new homes and refurbished some of the older houses. Your gran has joined in and tidied up her front garden. It's one of the prettiest in town this summer.' Kimberley pulled a face. It was hard to think of something nice to say about Gladys.

'That's good to hear, but I think it's hard for her by herself since my dad left to work in the mines a couple of years back. I figured I might come home for a while and help her out.'

'It would be lovely to see you,' Kimberley said. 'But how can I help you?'

'Well, I've applied for a job at the youth centre in Charleville, and I was hoping it's okay that I've put your name down as a referee. I meant to ring you earlier in the week, but I worked double shifts all week and I didn't get a chance. So, I really hope you don't mind because I put it in before I asked you. If it's a problem, tell me and I'll contact the convener and ask them to take your name off the list.'

'Tilly, no problem at all, that's fine. I'm happy to give you a character reference. We were such great mates back then, weren't we? It's such a shame we lost touch.'

'Yes, it is.'

'Which centre have you applied to, so I know who to expect to call?'

'The name of the person I've been dealing with is Rebecca Hunter.'

Kimberley nodded. 'I know Bec well. She's a good person, and I'll have no hesitation in giving you a reference. Actually, tonight is a surprise party for her birthday.'

'So you know her?'

Kimberley could hear the relief in Tilly's voice.

'I do.'

'Thank you so much, Kimberley. I truly appreciate it. It'll be great to catch up. Fingers crossed I can get out there, at least for an interview.'

'Well, I'll look forward to seeing you. If you do come to town for an interview, please make sure we catch up.' Kimberley frowned. 'How did you get my mobile? Not that I mind. Just curious.'

'It was a long shot. I asked Nana Tingle if you were back in town, and she said she had your number from some committee you were on together. Congratulations, by the way. I hear you're married to Quinn now..'

'I am. What about you? Married? Kids? Significant other?'

There was a bit of a quiet sigh at the end of the phone. 'Yep, life happens and often not the way we hoped. And no, I'm not married. Living the single life. No ties, so I can come home. I think it's time.'

'We'll certainly catch up. You won't know the town.'

'Kimberley? I just want to ask you one more thing. You might think I'm silly, but is Jeremy Johnson still in town?'

'Not that I know of, Tilly, and I'm sure I would've heard if he was. I actually haven't seen him since the end of high school, either. Last I heard, he was working as a nurse at St George. I remember Jacinta Mason mentioning that before she left town. Sophie was friends with him too.'

'It's great to hear all these familiar names. Did Sophie Cartwright marry Kent Mason?'

'She did.'

'That's not a surprise,' Tilly said. 'The

"couple most likely".'

Kimberley could hear the sadness in her voice. 'They were, but they've only married recently. Sophie was away for a while. And I don't know if you heard, but sadly, Julia Cartwright, Braden's wife, died in an accident a few years back, and Braden's now remarried. A lovely girl from Brisbane who came out to be the boys' nanny.'

'Braden and Julia had children?'

'Yes, I keep forgetting how long you've been gone. Three energetic boys. And Braden and Callie are here tonight too; they've got the most gorgeous almost one-year-old twins. There's been a lot of new people coming to town. It's a different place than what it was when we were at school, Tilly. It's a great place to live now. I do hope you get the job.'

'Me too. The Choice for Youth centre sounds like a good initiative from what Rebecca told me when I called to get the information pack. I like their philosophy statement.'

'There's a branch in Augathella and the centre is reaching out to other towns from what I've gathered since Bec's been involved. If I get a referee call or if Bec comes to see me, I'll talk you up. You were always good with the problem kids, even at school. Please stay in touch. I'll save your number in my contacts.'

'I will. Thank you so much, Kimberley. It *will* be good to see you again.'

'Bye for now.' Kimberley put her phone in her pocket and walked back to the dining room. She smiled at Gladys as she looked up at Kimberley curiously.

'I thought you were leaving already.' Gladys frowned. 'Seemed a bit rude.'

'No. I just had to take a phone call. How are you, Mrs Tingle?' she asked, not mentioning that she had just been speaking to her granddaughter.

'I'm well, thank you, Kimberley.'

'Hello, Beryl,' Kimberley smiled at the other woman sitting beside Gladys. Beryl was Gladys' constant companion around town.

Gladys frowned and looked at the old-fashioned watch on her wrist. 'How long before Rebecca gets here?' she said.

'I'm sure it won't be much longer. I think just about everyone is here.'

'It's way past my dinner time.'

Kimberley smiled. 'But think how good it will be to have a meal cooked for you and no washing up afterwards.' She could be diplomatic when she had to.

'I suppose. It's quite a big party. Is she turning forty?' Gladys asked.

'Don't be ridiculous, Gladys. Bec's not even thirty,' Beryl snapped. 'Not until in a few days anyway.'

Kimberley straightened as the conversations

in the room quietened. Matt moved away from the door with his finger to his lips. He'd asked everyone to try to keep the noise down so that when Bec arrived and was seated outside in the bistro by Sean—Matt had asked him to tell Bec he was running late and to put her at a table in there so she wouldn't get suspicious—she wouldn't hear familiar voices. He'd organised for one of the barmen to come in and take the drink orders and the door between the bistro and dining room was locked.

Kimberley smiled. Matt and Bec were so happy together; she wouldn't be surprised to see another Augathella wedding this year.

The town was growing, and she really hoped Tilly would come back, although putting up with Gladys might be a bit hard if she moved in with her. But Tilly had always been kind and had seen the best in everyone. Kimberley had been sincere when she'd said that she would be happy to give her a reference. Tilly was one of the most genuine women she'd ever known.

It would be good to see her again. Tilly had been a pretty eighteen-year-old, and like Sophie and Kent, she and Jeremy Johnson had been voted a "couple most likely" at the Year 12 formal, the year they had all finished school.

They'd both left town at the same time, and Kimberley hadn't seen either of them since. She'd been disappointed that they hadn't said goodbye, but at the end of the school year, everyone had been busy getting their plans in place. She'd often wondered if Tilly and Jeremy had stayed together, and she guessed she had her answer now.

CHAPTER 8

Matt was talking to Quinn at their table at their table when Kimberley made her way back. She shot him an apologetic smile. 'Sorry, Matt. I hope you weren't waiting for me. I just had a call come in. I thought it was work, but it wasn't.'

'No, we're waiting for Ben and Amelia to come back. Apparently, there was some drama in the car with Sebastian, and they had to go home and get a change of clothes.'

Callie smiled across the table. 'I can understand that. I believe Jenny had Sebastian at her place this morning, and she fed him pureed prunes for his dessert after his lunch and then sent him home. Apparently, the nappy he filled in the car on the way over was pretty spectacular.'

Kimberley pulled a face. 'Too much

information. I don't think I could cope with that. Give me kindergarten kids over babies any day.'

'You'll change your mind when you've got your own,' Callie said with a smile as she looked at Megan and Munro in their high chairs at the end of the table.

Matt waited until they finished speaking. 'Still be about ten minutes,' he said. 'So not a problem at all. Sean came in and told me that Bec is sitting quietly, having a drink, waiting for me to arrive. He told her that there's a function in here tonight and that I booked the table outside so we could be private.'

'As long as she doesn't get curious and comes to the door to see who's in here,' Callie said.

'No, Sean's locked the door to the bar. And we've all been pretty quiet. I must thank everyone when I can get on the microphone later.'

Kimberley's phone chimed again in her pocket, and she rolled her eyes. 'I'm sorry, this must be the call I'm waiting for. I'll be quick, and if I see Ben and Amelia arrive, I'll come back in with them,' she said to Matt with an apologetic smile before she hurried over to the side door and went out to the beer garden. 'Hello, Kimberley Calthorpe,' she said for the second time this afternoon.

'Hello, Kimberley.' This time an unfamiliar male voice greeted her.

'Yes, who's speaking, please?' Kimberley asked.

'I wonder if you remember me from high school. My name is Jeremy Johnson.'

Kimberley's eyes widened. 'Yes, Jeremy, of course I do. What can I do for you?'

Perhaps he knew that Tilly had called, but it seemed strange that she had asked after him.

'I was wondering if I could ask you a favour.

I'm coming back to live in Augathella. Or at least that's my plan.'

Kimberley listened carefully as he continued.

'I've applied for a job in Charleville. We were mates growing up. I was hoping I could ask you for a character reference.'

Kimberley nodded slowly. Until Tilly had moved to town in Year Ten, she and Jeremy had been very good mates, but they'd drifted apart as the romance between Tilly and Jeremy started. She and Tilly had spent a lot of time together in Years 11 and 12 when they'd chosen the same subjects. Many afternoons had been spent at Tilly's house when they planned to study, but usually ended up talking about fashion and bands.

'You're nursing, aren't you, Jeremy? Jacinta kept me up to date. Is the job at Charleville Hospital?'

'No. I'm leaving nursing. I took one break and worked in Melbourne for a few years, but I went back to St George and did my paediatric nursing pracs. I've decided to come back home for a while. My granddad is getting on, and he needs a bit of a hand on the farm, so I thought I'd see if I like living out there again and pick up a job at the same time.'

'So, what sort of job are you applying for?' Kimberley asked slowly. *Surely not,* it would be too much of a coincidence, she thought.

'Apparently, the community centre down at Charleville, Choice for Youth, is looking for a couple of new youth workers. I saw it in our public service gazette, applied, and I've got my work referees from Melbourne, but I was hoping that someone with a bit of knowledge of me as a local might put in a good word for me. I thought of you straightaway, Kim. Even though it's been a long time since I left town.'

'Of course, Jeremy. I don't know anything about your work since you left, but I'd be more than happy to give you a character reference. You mentioned a couple of youth workers. Is there more than one position coming up?' she asked.

'I believe they're looking for a number of new youth workers. The convenor told me about some funding grant when I called to enquire about the job. So I'd like to throw my hat in the ring and hope I've got a chance of coming home.'

'Ten years, a long time to still consider it home.'

'Yes, but I think where you're born and spend your school years is always home, no matter how long you're gone, don't you? What about you, Kimberley? What are you doing these days?'

'I'm the assistant principal at our primary

school,' Kimberley said.

'Married?'

'Yes.'

'Kids?'

'No kids. What about you, Jeremy?' Maybe she could get to the bottom of why Tilly was asking if he was still in town. Was it a conflict of interest to give a reference for two people applying for the same job? She'd have to ask Bec. But not tonight.

'No, single. Free as a bird. Hope you don't mind me asking all the personal questions. We always got on well, didn't we?'

'We did. From our first day of kindergarten.'

'I've never been ready to settle down, much to the disappointment of several women.' His chuckle came across the phone, and Kimberley remembered it well. Jeremy had always been a smiler. He had always been the happy one in the group and was always able to lift anyone who was a bit down. 'Do I sound big-headed saying that?'

'Not at all. I know you well enough.' Kimberley swallowed. Even though it had been a long time, she felt she knew Jeremy well enough to ask. 'Do you mind me asking about Tilly? I thought you were heading off to get married?'

There was quiet for a while, and she wondered if she had overstepped.

'A long story there, Kimberley. And not a pretty one. One for a night over a good bottle of red. Do you know where Tilly is these days? I hope she's happy. She deserves to be.'

Kimberley swallowed again as she thought quickly. She was damned if she did and damned if she didn't.

'Last I heard, she was in Brisbane. Anyway, look, I have to go, Jeremy, and yes, I'm more than happy to be your referee. When or if I get the call, I'll let you know. Got your number in my phone now.'

'Thanks, Kim. I knew I could depend on you. Hopefully, we'll catch up soon.'

Kimberley walked across the beer garden, thoughtful again. Should she ring Tilly and let her know that Jeremy applied for the job too, or should she just let things take their natural course?

Never one to interfere, she realised it wasn't up to her to decide. She'd be breaching confidentiality if she did.

If Bec asked her to be a referee for both of them, she would, and she'd think carefully about what to say.

It had turned into an interesting night. Ben and Amelia pulled up as she was about to go inside, and she waited for them by the door.

'Bit of a nappy drama, I hear,' she said with a grin.

Ben was actually a bit pale. 'Oh my God, don't even talk about it. I'm going to have a word with my mother about feeding Sebastian prunes. Never again! It was right up into his—'

Kimberley put a hand up. 'Too much information, you guys. I don't need to know.'

But Amelia finished Ben's sentence for him. 'The contents of his nappy had gone right up to the back of his neck and into his hair.' She smiled down at her now-clean baby. 'We had to give him a bath.'

'Oh yuk, gross. I won't be able to eat now,' Kimberley said.

'Not prunes for dessert, anyway.' Ben laughed at the look on Kimberley's face as they followed her in.

'You'll keep, Ben Riley,' she said.

Matt was standing by the other door and gave them a thumbs-up as they walked in. Kimberley went over and sat with Quinn. Matt spoke quietly as everyone stopped talking.

'Everyone ready?' he asked.

The room was quiet as everyone smiled and nodded. Pointing to the side door, Matt indicated he was going that way.

That way, Bec wouldn't wonder why he was coming out of the private function room, Kimberley thought.

'Be back with her in five. Lights out when Sean gives you the nod from the bar?' he said.

Kimberley stood by the light switch and nodded as conversations resumed quietly. She couldn't wait to see the look on Bec's face. It was going to be a good night. Chloe caught her eye from two tables away, smiling with anticipation.

Kimberley scanned the room. All of Bec's friends were here tonight, including the four new couples in town: the Cartwrights, with their five children; Dr Harry and Laura, heads close together, looking like two lovebirds; Sophie and

Kent; Fallon and Jon, and their respective children. Jenna and Josh Foley were at the table with Chloe and her friends, and most of the teachers from the primary school and the staff from the hospital filled two long tables at the back of the room. The only close friends missing were Jacinta and Ryan Francesco, who had moved to Brisbane.

Sean gave her a nod, and Kimberley flicked the light switch.

CHAPTER 9

Tilly Tingle - Brisbane

Tilly sat on the bench of the sheltered area as she waited for the next river cat to arrive and give her a ride back to her apartment. It had been a good conversation with Kimberley, and she was relieved to hear that Jeremy had left Augathella. She didn't want to ask too many questions in case Kimberley wondered why she was so curious.

She wondered if Jeremy's family had also left town, but she quickly pushed that thought out of her mind. All she could do was hope.

In any case, Tilly had left town and hadn't been back since. If it weren't for Nana needing her, she would never have considered going back. The memories associated with Augathella were difficult to face. Six months ago, Nana had surprised her with a phone call asking her to come home. She'd finished her studies in the months since Nana had called and worked on building her courage.

Tilly and Nana had always had a close relationship, despite Nana's occasionally abrasive demeanour. Tilly knew Nana had her reasons for being that way; she hadn't had an easy life, especially after losing Pop when Tilly was just a baby. Tilly only hoped she wouldn't become bitter like Nana.

All Tilly wanted in life was a happy relationship and someone to love—just as she had back in high school. It seemed she was bad at forming relationships. Every relationship she'd had since Jeremy had ended in failure, and she knew most of the time, it had been her fault. No one ever measured up to him.

Or measured up to the Jeremy that she had known until he had let her down.

So when Nana asked for help, she was more than happy to provide it, even though it had taken her a while to organise herself.

Tilly knew the thought of the Johnsons still being in Augathella had stopped her from moving back for the past six months, but she'd finally convinced herself that if they were there, she would deal with it.

At least she knew now that Jeremy wasn't there; it would make the move a lot easier. All she had to do was get a job.

She'd wondered about him over the years as she moved from job to job, and city to city, never being able to settle. She knew she'd suffered emotionally dealing with the situation when she left, but she didn't imagine that ten years later, it would still be impacting her decision-making.

Tilly had actually felt sick at the thought of moving when Nana had first asked her, but her grandmother's plea had finally won her over, and she'd put in her notice at her most recent casual job in the bar in the Valley.

Nana was always interested in what she was doing when they had their fortnightly call and where Tilly was working. Her grandmother told Tilly she was living an adventurous life. Maybe working on a cruise boat in Cairns, working in a bar in the city, and, in between jobs when she saved up enough, travelling overseas to what Nana always said were exotic locations had sounded adventurous.

But Nana always ended the conversation with, 'Don't you think it's time to get a real job and settle down, Matilda?'

Tilly's preferred destinations had been third-world countries. She had been taken aback by the poverty and the children begging in many of the places she'd visited, and the experiences had awakened a need in her.

She wanted to help. If she couldn't be happy,

maybe she could get a job where she was helping others. Two years ago, when she had been working at the bar in the Valley, she picked up a casual position at a community centre working with troubled young adults. She worked there for a few weeks as a volunteer, and she'd fitted in so well that Chris, her boss, had asked her to come and work in a paid position at the drop-in centre two nights a week. Her Friday and Saturday nights for the last two years had been spent there. It wasn't pretty; she encountered many kids with drug and alcohol addiction and some who had been sexually assaulted, but Tilly loved her work. She finally felt she was making a difference and was doing something worthwhile. So Chris had recommended the course for her to enrol in, and she'd graduated with flying colours about three weeks ago.

Seeing the job in the Charleville paper last week was a sign for her. She could go and live with Nana Tingle and continue the work she loved.

If she got the job.

If she was going to live with Nana, there was no way she could stay home with her all day. She had a car, so if she was successful, it wouldn't be a problem to travel down to Charleville for however many days she had to work.

Tilly doubted herself, but she knew she had a good chance of success, based on the brilliant reference Chris had given her for her work, her outstanding results in her Certificate IV in Youth Work course, and hopefully, with a bit of a local push from Kimberley. She just had to get her head together, forget about her Augathella history, and try to present her best side if she got to interview.

The river cat appeared around the bend of the river, and Tilly stood up. If she didn't get the position, she'd make the best of it. She was sure

she could find a job in Augathella or Charleville,
but working as a youth worker where she grew
up would be a way to redeem herself.

Be positive, she told herself.

CHAPTER 10

Bec - 29th February

Bec smiled at Sean as he came into the bar and went to the wine fridge at the far end. He lifted out three bottles of champagne and hurried back out of sight. Bec wondered what the function was in the dining room tonight; she hadn't heard of anything in town. Maybe it was a work do, or maybe it was a group of tourists. She noticed quite a few vans parked down at the recreation centre at the free camp a couple of days ago. She was surprised at how quiet the rest of the pub was tonight. None of the usual locals were there, even though she did realise it was past drinks time and all of the road workers, mine workers, and station workers that often called in for a beer on their way home would've been gone by now. The only person in the bar was an elderly lady sitting by the door, reading a magazine, someone she didn't recognise.

The pub was barely recognisable these days compared to what it had been this time last year. The old timber wall in the bistro had been relined with plaster and painted a warm copper colour. Chloe and Rosie had found pieces of old farm equipment and implements, and they hung from the ceiling in various places and were on the top of the new corner cupboards that were in each corner of the bar. The old chipped wooden tables and chairs had gone, and there was modern furniture in the bistro. They'd managed to source some old-fashioned bar stools, and there were a dozen or so along the length of the bar that really fit in with the old-world look. The original bar had been sanded back and polished to a deep shine. She recalled a conversation with Reg, the town icon who had sadly passed away last year. He told her the history of the pub and how the timber in the bar had come from a local property back in the early 1900s; she was pleased to see that there was still a chair out the front with a little black plaque in remembrance of Reg.

She was disappointed that she couldn't peek in the dining room; she was keen to see what had been done there too.

Bec glanced at her watch. It was only a couple of minutes past seven, so with Matt's usual tardiness, he could still be a while. She waited till Sean came back into the bar, and she walked over with her empty glass. 'Would you like another drink, Bec?'

'Maybe a soft drink?' she said, and then she reconsidered. 'Yes, why not? It's my birthday week. I'll have another wine, thanks, Sean, but I'll sit on it over dinner too. What are the specials on the menu tonight?'

Sean shook his head. 'I'm not sure if the new chef's got any specials on tonight, just the usual

99

weeknight menu. I think chicken pie's in the—'

'Okay, the usual is good. Whatever it is.'

Sean poured her wine. 'Just a small one,' she said, and he filled it to the line that came halfway up the glass. 'Thank you, Sean. Looks like you're busy tonight. Matt shouldn't be long. We'll order quickly and won't stay late.'

'Yes, big crowd. I'd better get back in there.' He kept glancing nervously at the closed door at the end of the bar.

'Thank you.' Bec made her way back to the table and sat. It was lovely to sit down and have some headspace; she forced herself to stop worrying about the rain. It was beautiful here tonight. She had good applications for the youth worker's position, and she should hear back about her grant any day now.

When she bumped into them in IGA yesterday, Chloe and Rosie told her that the building work was going really well, and she had organised to go out there for a look in the next week or so.

Her main worry now was that Easter was early this year, and today was the twenty-ninth; she had four weeks and two days to get everything sorted. She drew a deep breath and tried to relax as a bit of tension started to filter in. 'It will be fine,' she told herself.

The main door pushed open, and her smile widened as Matt stepped into the bistro. Her breath caught; she would never get tired of looking at him, and tonight he'd made a special effort. If she didn't know better, she'd say he had new clothes on. She hadn't recalled seeing those before or in their wardrobe; his jeans were black, with a shiny belt and a pale blue shirt. As he walked over, she noticed the glossy shine on his boots.

Matt paused beside an elderly woman who was sitting alone. He leaned down, put his hand on her shoulder, and spoke to her. She looked up at him, smiled, and nodded. He stepped back as she rose, took the woman's hand, and led her out the door.

Bec frowned. What on earth was he doing? Perhaps she'd broken down and had been waiting for a lift, and Matt had offered to help. Perhaps not.

He was back within a minute or so, and warmth curled in her stomach as he met her gaze. Matt was in need of a haircut, but the longer curls touching the back of his neck suited him. His smile was just for her. His beautiful eyes lit up, and a wave of love warmed Bec. She loved this man more than she'd ever thought was possible.

Matt didn't sit down. His hand cupped the back of her neck as he leaned down, and his lips took hers in a slow, tender kiss. 'You look absolutely beautiful, sweetheart.'

'You look good, too. I'm so pleased you got

dressed up for me. New clothes?'

'It's a special night, babe, not often a young lady turns thirty. I'm sorry we couldn't do it on Saturday night, on your birthday.'

'You know, I think this is nicer. It's not crowded here tonight, and it's just you and me. That makes it special.'

Matt kept standing beside her, his smile wide.

'Are you going to sit down?' she asked. 'Sean should be back in a moment to get you a drink. I didn't order you one because I thought you'd be a lot later.'

'You know me well, don't you?'

'I do.' She reached up and squeezed his hand. 'Who was the lady at the door?' she asked curiously.

'She used to work at IGA.'

Bec raised her eyebrows; that didn't tell her much. She shrugged. Matt seemed preoccupied.

'Sit down,' she said.

'Do you want another drink, or do you want to eat first? I thought we might go in and order now.'

'Go in?' Bec frowned, 'I thought we were eating out here. There's a private function in the dining room. Sean's been run off his feet.'

'There's room for us. I made sure.'

Her physical attraction to Matt was overwhelming. Even though they'd been together for over a year, that lazy smile always sent her heart racing. Bec made an instant decision; she'd put it off too long. She'd let life get in the way, and it was time she got her priorities right. She reached up and grabbed his hand.

'Matt, sit down for a minute. I want to ask you something.'

'Okay, you're not too hungry?'

'I am, but not for food. I want to tell you how

much I love you.'

'That goes without saying.' His fingers curled around hers. 'I love you too, Bec Hunter.'

'Sit down, Matt.'

'Yes, ma'am.' He obliged, still holding her hand.

'Do you know what date it is?'

'Nope,' he said with a grin. Despite being an accountant and focusing on figures and numbers all day long, Matt rarely knew what day of the week it was. 'I do know it's your birthday in a couple of days, so let me work it out. Your birthday's the third of March.' Bec grinned as he counted back on his fingers. 'So that makes today the twenty-eighth of February.'

She shook her head. 'No, it's the twenty-ninth of February today.'

'Oh, I forgot it was a leap year.' He squeezed her fingers.

'Matt, do you know what that means?'

'It means that I haven't done my spreadsheets properly for my clients. What did you want to ask me? We probably need to go to our table.'

She laughed. 'In a minute. No, Matt, do you know what can happen on the twenty-ninth of February?'

He shook his head, looking confused.

Bec took a deep breath, and put her other hand on his. They were the only ones in the room and all was quiet. Sean wasn't behind the bar, and the refrigerator filled the silence. A murmur of conversation came in from the dining room occasionally, but they were in their own world.

'It's a month until Easter,' she said, 'but I don't want to wait that long.'

Confusion crossed his face. 'For your camp?'

'No, for what we talked about. What I was waiting for.'

Matt nodded slowly as he realised what she meant.

'Hang on,' she said before he could say anything. 'Matt Randall, I love you to the moon and back, and I want to spend the rest of my life with you.' A smile crept across her face as she held his eyes. 'Will you marry me, Matt?' she said.

His mouth dropped open and widened. Matt dropped her hands and jumped to his feet. He reached out and took Bec's hands again and pulled her up beside him. His arms went around her, and he rested his cheek against hers.

'Did you just propose to me, Bec?'

'I did. I took advantage of it being the one day of the year when a woman can propose to their man. Are you going to answer me?' she said.

'It would give me the greatest pleasure to accept your proposal.' His fingers lifted her chin, and his lips took her in a tender kiss.

'I preempted you,' she murmured against his mouth.

Matt leaned back, and his eyes held hers. 'Yes, I was intending to ask you again on your birthday, even though you told me to wait until Easter. I didn't think it was the sort of thing we could put a date on. And for me, tonight we are celebrating your birthday, so I came prepared. But, Bec?' His voice shook with emotion. 'You asking me has just filled me with more happiness than I ever thought I could feel.'

Matt moved away, reached into his shirt pocket, and pulled out a small royal blue box. Bec looked at him as he flipped open the box, and the brilliant shine of a single diamond caught the light from above.

'I intended getting down on one knee after dinner tonight, but you've beaten me, so I guess I don't have to ask before I put my ring on your finger,' he said, his eyes filled with love.

Bec held out her left hand, her eyes filling with tears as Matt slid the perfectly fitting ring onto her ring finger.

'I guess we're formally engaged now,' he said, his beautiful smile as wide as she'd ever seen it. His arms went around her again, and it was just as well they were alone in the bar. There was no sign of Sean yet.

'Now that was going to be for later,' he said, 'but I'm so happy that we sorted that now. I've got a surprise for you, too,' he said.

'Have you bought me a birthday cake?' she replied with a grin.

The door opened, and Sean reappeared behind the bar.

'Table set in there for us?' Matt asked.

'There is, Matt. I'll just open the door for you,' he said.

Matt took Bec's hand and held it tightly, but

she kept lifting her left hand and looking at the ring. She'd never forget the look in his eyes when she proposed to him.

'You like it?' he said.

'I love it. When did you get it?'

'I've had it for about three months. I got it when we went to Brisbane before Christmas.'

'You're good at keeping secrets,' she said. Matt put his hand on her back and showed her through the door that Sean had opened ahead of him.

The room was quiet now and in darkness, as Bec turned to Matt in confusion. 'Are you sure the dining room's open?'

'I am.' Suddenly the lights came on, and cries of surprise filled the room. Bec looked around, the room was full. It didn't register for a moment that they were all people she knew. Matt nudged her and pointed to the right of the room, and her mouth dropped open as she saw the huge

'Happy Birthday, Bec' banner strung along the sidewall.

'Happy birthday, my love,' he said.

She put a hand to her mouth. 'Oh my God, Matt, you, you—what, I don't know—oh, thank you. I had no idea.'

'I did pretty good, I think. But the surprise you've given me tonight beats this.' Matt put his arm around her as the room quieted. 'Hey everyone, I have to tell you what's just happened. It's a pretty special night for us. Not only is it Bec's birthday, and we're all celebrating with her tonight.' He looked down at her, and his eyes were filled with love. 'But this beautiful woman just proposed to me.' He held up her left hand and smiled around the room. 'And I accepted. So, as well as being a birthday party, let's turn tonight into an engagement party!'

Everyone stood and clapped, and Bec realised how much she loved living in this community. Chloe and Rosie were the first to hug them both.

'Congratulations, you guys! What a fabulous surprise.'

The Ingrams and the Masons weren't far behind. Jon and then Kent shook Matt's hand and reached over to kiss Bec's cheek.

'Congratulations,' they said as Sophie stepped closer and hugged her tightly.

'So happy for you, Bec. You couldn't have picked a better man.' Sophie chuckled. 'And I *love* that you proposed to him.'

'I think champagne is in order,' Braden Cartwright's voice came from behind them. 'My shout, Matt. A bottle for every table.'

'Braden, you don't have to do that,' Matt said.

'Oh yes, I do, mate. I know exactly how you're feeling.' He put his arm around Callie, who stood behind him. 'I think this will be one of the happiest nights of your life. I wish you both a happy life.'

Bec's eyes filled with tears as she saw the look on Callie's face as she looked up at her husband. She knew they'd had some tough times, but if it hadn't been for little Petie Cartwright, Bec knew she probably wouldn't be standing here engaged to the man that she loved. She reached up and kissed Braden's cheek. 'Thank you, Braden. That's very generous of you.'

Callie squeezed her hands. 'I am so happy for you. What a night! Whoever would've thought that a Thursday night in Augathella could be filled with so much joy?'

She looked down as Petie pushed his way between Matt and Bec. He held out his hand to Matt and shook his hand.

'Congratulations, Matt,' he said. Callie's eyes met Bec's, and Callie ruffled Petie's hair. 'That was lovely of you, Petie. Very grown-up, my little man.'

Petie turned to Bec and said, 'You'll have to bend down so I can kiss your cheek, Bec.'

Bending down, Pete whispered in her ear, 'He's a very good man, Matt Randall is, so you take care of him, won't you, Bec?'

Bec put her arms around Petie and squeezed him. 'He thinks you're pretty special too, Petie, and yes, I will look after him very well.'

'When will you have kids?' the little boy asked. 'That usually happens after people get married?'

Bec chuckled. 'Yes, but maybe not straight away.'

'Well, Matt's been sort of like a bit of a special person to me, so when you do have kids, I'll be good friends with them,' Petey said. 'They'll sort of be like half-brothers to me, I think.'

'I think you're getting ahead of yourself

there, mate,' Braden said.

'But what a lovely sentiment,' Matt said. 'Thank you, Petie. You're pretty special to me too, mate. Forget this handshaking.' He reached down and lifted Petie up, and gave him a massive hug.

A stream of well-wishers surrounded them and congratulations went on for about fifteen minutes, and Bec felt totally surrounded by love. Even Gladys Tingle came up and hugged her.

Finally, Sean came out and said to Matt, 'The chef's getting anxious in there. He's got a few special sauces and things simmering on the stove, and he's wondering when everyone's ready to eat.'

Matt grinned. 'There's a very special menu tonight, Bec. No chicken Parmis for you. I hope you weren't depending on one for your dinner.'

Matt led Bec to the table near the bar, and she smiled as she saw how beautifully the table was set. Sean had somehow managed to find a plastic bride and groom, which now took pride of place in the middle of the table.

'Thank you, Sean. Where on earth did you find that?'

'You'd be surprised what we've got out in the back room,' Sean said. 'Now, would you like chicken or beef, guys?'

The evening was full of happiness and hilarity. Bec was overwhelmed again when, after dinner, Sean lifted a cloth off a table in the corner of the room that was filled with presents.

'Oh, you guys—you're so naughty! You didn't need to buy me birthday presents.'

'Now we have to get you engagement presents too,' Ben Riley called out.

'No, you won't. Don't be silly. Leave it for the wedding,' she said.

'When is the wedding?' Ben called out. 'You're not going to elope, are you? It's about time we had a wedding in town again.'

Kimberley and Quinn Calthorpe looked at each other and smiled. They'd surprised everybody by eloping.

Bec leaned over and kissed Matt as they took their seats.

'Thank you. This is a lovely surprise. Everyone I care about is here.' She grinned at him and nodded to a table a couple of rows away where the woman Matt had spoken to at the door was sitting beside Gladys Tingle and Beryl. 'Even some I don't know.'

'She looked lonely,' he said.

'You're a good man, Matt Randall, and I love you.' Bec held her hand out and gazed at her engagement ring.

CHAPTER 11

Tilly

Tilly smoothed her hands down the front of her dress as she made her way to the chair in the waiting room of the Shire Council chambers at Charleville. She wasn't usually one to dress up, preferring to spend her time in jeans and T-shirts, but to look professional, she'd bought a navy dress before she left Brisbane and pressed it in the motel room this morning. She hadn't expected to feel so nervous, and it made her realise how much she wanted this job. She deliberately hadn't been to see her grandmother yet because she didn't want to get her hopes up. She would wait and see how long it would be after the interview before she knew if she was successful or not. Depending on that answer, she might go up to Augathella in the next day or two.

In the meantime, she was going to play tourist. She was fascinated by the World War II exhibition that she'd read about and also by the star viewing at the Cosmos Centre. She'd have no trouble filling in a few days, and then she'd go up and see Nana Tingle.

She was the only one in the waiting room, and she wondered how many applicants there were. She imagined they would be spaced half an hour apart so they wouldn't see each other in the waiting room. There would be nothing more embarrassing than talking to someone else who was going for the same job as you before you went in for your interview.

The door opened, and she looked up as a dark-haired woman walked into the waiting room.

'Hello, I'm assuming you're Tilly Tingle,' she said.

'Yes,' Tilly confirmed. 'I am.'

'Welcome, Tilly. I'm Bec Hunter. Come on through.'

Another woman stood from the table where she was sitting as Tilly and Bec walked into the room. 'Tilly, this is my assistant, Alice Templeton.'

'Please sit down,' Alice said. 'Would you like a glass of water?'

'Yes, please. My throat is a bit dry from nerves,' Tilly said.

'Don't be nervous. We've read your application, and we've seen the results of your course. You've done very well, and your two referees spoke very highly of you too.'

'And being an Augathella local means that you know the district,' Alice added.

'Yes, I understand how these positions work. I hope I have met all the criteria,' Tilly said.

By the time the interview was over, her nerves had completely gone; she'd settled into more of a conversation than an interview. Bec and Alice were professional and easy to talk to.

'Thanks so much for coming in today. Are you staying in town very long? I see that you have a Brisbane address,' Bec noted.

'I did have a Brisbane address, but I've actually left there. I really have no fixed address at the moment,' Tilly chuckled. 'I'm going up to Augathella later in the week, and I'll stay with my grandmother. But in the interim, if you need to contact me, just call my mobile.'

'Do you have any questions?' Bec asked.

'Just the usual one that I'm sure you're used to getting in interviews,' Tilly said. 'I'm just wondering how long it would be before you make a decision.'

'Well, we've already read all of the applications and called all the referees, so once we finish interviewing today, we're hoping that we come to a decision this afternoon or first thing in the morning. So, you'll get a call either way, say, by lunchtime tomorrow. Does that suit you, Tilly?'

'That's really good, thank you,' Tilly said, feeling relieved.

'I can't promise anything. And we're very appreciative that you've come from Brisbane to be interviewed.' Bec nodded and smiled.

'We are,' Alice agreed.

Tilly stood and shook both their hands, feeling good. Even if she didn't get the job, she'd given it her best shot.

***

Jeremy Johnson glanced at his phone to check the time as he locked the car door. He stifled a yawn and hoped being tired wouldn't impact his performance at the interview today. He'd worked the night shift at the hospital in St. George last night and grabbed about four hours of sleep before leaving early to drive up to

Charleville.

He checked into a motel room on arrival and got a curious look from the receptionist. 'Are you going to stay the night too, or just use the room for the day?'

He grinned to himself; he knew what she was thinking. Singe bloke, early daytime only booking at a motel.

'It depends,' he said. 'I've got a job interview today. I've just driven up a long way for it.'

Her cheeks flushed, and he grinned again. 'I will probably come back here afterwards and have a sleep, and then I'll see whether I'll be driving back tonight or not or whether I'll stay.'

'Thank you, Mr Johnson.' She handed over the room key. 'Room 17, up the steps and along to the right. Thank you.'

Jeremy was aware of the interest in her eyes, and he thought what a pretty girl she was, but his focus was on the upcoming interview.

He put the car keys in his pocket after locking his car and crossed the road, heading towards the council chambers where the interview was being held. As he passed the museum, three doors away from the building, a young woman walked down the steps of the council building, turned onto the street and walked away from him.

It was Tilly.

The minute Jeremy saw her step out of the door, he stopped. She must have moved back to the district. The last thing he needed was to see Tilly Tingle this morning. He couldn't afford to let his emotions get tangled. He really wanted this job in Charleville, but he also would appreciate the chance to finally talk to Tilly. There was so much unresolved between them. Jeremy hesitated and then made up his mind. He broke into a light jog, ran past the steps and in her direction.

'Tilly!' he called out as he was close behind her. Her shoulders tensed and she walked faster without turning. It was clear she recognised his voice.

'Tilly!' he called a second time.

She stopped and turned slowly. Tilly Tingle, the girl he had fallen in love with at seventeen, looked no different to than she had ten years ago. The same as she looked in the dreams he still had about her, and the same as she did in the photo that was still in his wallet; the photo that had caused comments with the couple of women he had attempted to have a relationship with.

'Jeremy.' Her voice caught as she looked at him, her beautiful hazel eyes wide.

'Hello, Tilly. It's been a long time.'

Her throat worked as she swallowed, and she struggled to answer him.

'It has. What are you doing in Charleville?'

'I've got an appointment,' he replied.

'Oh. I won't hold you up then.' She began to move away from him; it was clear she didn't want to speak to him.

'No. Wait. I've got a few minutes to spare. I'd really like to speak to you. Could you meet me in a little while?'

She hesitated, then sighed. 'I suppose I could wait.'

'Good. Where can we meet?'

'There's a coffee shop in the next block, on the other side of the road. I'll meet you there at 11.15.' She glanced down at the gold watch on her left wrist. 'I haven't got much time. If you're not there by 11:30, I'll be gone.'

'I'll be there,' he said. 'Thank you, Tilly.'

He resisted watching her as she walked away, and he realised that no matter how long it had been, she was still a part of him. She always had been, and Jeremy knew she always would be.

Even if it had only been a teenage romance—and he knew it had been more than that—Tilly would always be a part of him.

He walked up the steps of the council chambers and into the front foyer, trying to get Tilly out of his mind and focus on the interview ahead. The receptionist at the counter looked at him with a smile. 'May I help you?'

'Yes, I have an appointment with Bec Hunter at 10:30,' he said.

'Take a seat,' she said. 'I'll let Bec know you're here.'

Despite not being one hundred percent focused on the interview, Jeremy thought he had done okay. He probably could've done better, but he answered all the questions, and Bec and Alice, the interviewers, commented on his excellent references. He stood as the interview finished and shook both their hands.

'Are you heading back to St. George today?'

Bec asked.

'I'm not sure yet. I don't have to go back to work at the hospital for a couple of days, so I might hang around town for a while. I've booked into a motel,' he said.

'That sounds good. We'll be giving you a call tomorrow by lunchtime at the latest, Jeremy,' Alice said with a smile.

'Thank you. I'll look forward to it.'

He pulled out his phone and glanced at the clock on the wall again as he left. He hoped he hadn't been too obvious; his eyes had flicked to the clock on the wall of the interview room a number of times during the interview. He'd tried to focus on the questions, but in the back of his mind the whole time, was Tilly Tingle waiting for him at the coffee shop.

The door closed behind him, and he picked up his pace as he crossed the foyer, went through the door, and hurried down the steps. He turned right and headed up the street before crossing at the pedestrian crossing and then crossing the main highway. He spotted the coffee shop that Tilly had mentioned; it was 11:10. He'd been gone for just under forty-five minutes, so hopefully, she was still there, and she hadn't had second thoughts.

It was past the morning coffee time and not yet time for the lunch trade, so the coffee shop was quite empty. A mother with a pram sat at the corner table reading a book as her child slept. Tilly was sitting facing the door on the other side of the coffee shop, a cup in front of her.

Jeremy walked over. 'Thanks for meeting me, Tilly. I appreciate it. Would you like another drink? I'm going to get a coffee.' He needed the caffeine to concentrate when he spoke to her.

'Yes, thanks. A chai tea would be good.' Her face was expressionless, and her tone flat, and Jeremy wondered what the hell he was going to say. There was so much he needed to say, so much he wanted to tell her, but he didn't want to blow it by rushing in. First, he wanted to find out where she lived and what she was doing.

No matter how hard he'd tried to find her on social media or asking friends over the years, Tilly had disappeared into thin air when she'd left him ten years ago.

Overnight.

When Jeremy discovered why she'd left town, guilt and regret had filled him. He should have stood up to his parents, but at nineteen, it had been hard to buck the rigid environment he had grown up in.

That day had been the beginning of the end of his relationship with his parents. He'd never forgiven them for what they'd done, but his greatest regret was that he hadn't gone to see Tilly as soon as he'd heard what had happened that night. Dad had forbidden him to leave the house, and foolishly Jeremy had obeyed. By the time he'd gone to see her the next morning, she'd already left, and he hadn't been able to find her. Her parents wouldn't tell him where she'd gone; they would barely speak to him. He'd obviously been lumped in the same basket as his parents.

Even though he had only been nineteen, he'd known Tilly was the woman for him. Age had nothing to do with it; he'd known she'd felt the same. Tilly had set the bar so high no other woman had ever measured up, no matter how hard he'd tried to forget her. He had to talk to her, ask her to forgive him, make sure she was happy, and he would be able to get on with his life.

Now here she was sitting in front of him, as pretty as ever, and Jeremy was tongue-tied.

More than pretty; she had grown into a beautiful woman. During the interview, all he could think of was Tilly standing on the footpath in her navy blue dress, looking at him as though he'd crawled out from under a stone.

Well, he had half an hour or so to sort it out and seek forgiveness from the woman he'd loved.

***

Jeremy was directly in Tilly's line of sight as he stood at the counter ordering the two hot drinks. Even though she was sure the waitress would bring them over, Jeremy waited until they were made and then carried them over himself.

That pause gave Tilly a little time to compose herself; seeing Jeremy again, looking into his eyes, and hearing his voice had thrown her into a spin. Her usual serenity was long gone.

She tried to bring back those feelings of anger she had carried for so long before she finally pushed them away a few years later.

The problem was even though she had been angry, losing Jeremy from her life had left her empty. She'd tried to fill it with work and travel, and it had taken a long time before her heartache had eased.

She knew what carrying anger had done to her mother, even though Dad had tried to tell her that the cancer that took her mother at a far too young age had been there before the incident with the Johnsons. Tilly had always blamed his parents, and to a certain extent, she blamed Jeremy himself. He hadn't done anything to stop what was said, the rumours that circulated. She would never forgive him for that. All she'd wanted to do was forget about it and move on with her life.

His hands shook as he put her tea in front of her and then walked around the table to sit opposite her. He reached for the spoon, his eyes on his cup, before eventually lifting his head to hold her gaze.

'It's good to see you, Tilly. It's been a very

long time,' he said.

'It has,' she replied, keeping her voice expressionless.

'I tried to find you, you know, but you were gone, and no one would tell me where you were.'

She shrugged. 'I moved away. It was necessary. I had no choice.'

'I know, but I should've done something. I should've looked harder for you. But more than anything, I should have come over that night.'

'Jeremy, can I just ask you one thing?'

'Yes, of course,' he said slowly.

'It's all in the past; it's been ten years. We've moved on. We're different people now and we don't see each other, so I can't see any point in discussing what happened. It's all water under the bridge. It's nice to see you and say hello, but let's leave it at that, shall we?'

He held her gaze for a few seconds before nodding slowly. 'Well, if that's what you need, I guess all I can do is tell you I'm sorry, give you my apology, and hope that you'll accept it.'

'I accept your apology, okay? I have to go now.'

'Wait, you haven't drunk your tea, and I want to know a little bit about you. I want to know that you're happy, Tilly.'

She picked up her tea; it was so hot she burnt her tongue trying to drink it too fast. She picked up the napkin from the saucer and dabbed her lips.

'I'm happy,' she said, hoping he couldn't hear the untruth in her expression. Happy? She'd forgotten what that felt like when he had let her down.

'I'm pleased. Where do you live these days?' he asked.

'I live in Brisbane,' she said, deciding not to tell him she had moved back to the Murweh district in case he was still around. God, she hoped he wasn't. That was the last thing she needed—Jeremy Johnson in town. If that was the case, she wouldn't be accepting the job if it was offered.

She pushed that thought away. As soon as she said she had forgiven him, maybe she could move on. 'What about you? Where do you live?'

'I live down in St. George,' he said. 'Just had to come up here for the day. I'm a nurse. I went to uni in Brisbane. Shame we didn't run into each other there a little bit sooner.'

'I haven't always lived there. I've been around,' she said.

'What sort of work do you do?' he asked. 'Did you do the teaching degree you'd applied for?'

'No.' Her voice was clipped. 'A bit of uni, waitressing, some travelling.'

'I—'

Tilly cut him off. 'I have to go now.'

She was sure he could see the lack of interest she forced into her expression. It was as though they had never been more than casual acquaintances. She blew on her tea before drinking it quickly and setting the cup down.

'Well, it has been nice to see you,' she tried to be as polite as she could. 'Maybe we'll run into each other again one day.'

'I hope so, Tilly. It's been good to see you, and thank you for letting me apologise to you.'

She shrugged again and stood, smoothing down the fabric of her dress. She picked up her bag. 'Thanks for the tea. See you around. Bye.'

As she walked to the door, she knew his eyes were on her.

CHAPTER 12

Bec

Bec sat down, staring at the diamond ring on her finger, still unable to believe that she had proposed to Matt last night. Even though she had known it was February twenty-nine, she'd had no intention of doing so. When he walked in with that gorgeous, sexy smile, the idea had come rocketing in. Now, she couldn't help but smile every time she looked at the glinting stone on her left hand.

'Stop looking at that ring,' Alice said with a grin. 'Although I couldn't be happier for you, Bec, I can't believe you proposed. When you and Matt walked into the dining room last night, I knew something had happened. You were both glowing.'

'Neither can I, but it was the right time.

Anyway,' Bec said briskly, pulling some papers on the desk towards her, 'we've got a decision to make. So tell me what you think, okay? I've decided which two of the five I would like to select,' Bec said.

'There were two standout candidates for me too. Let's see if our decisions correspond,' Alice commented. 'Who did you choose?'

'Well, Tilly Tingle and Jeremy Johnson were the top two candidates for me. As well as having local backgrounds, they were outstanding. Nothing to do with being from the local area, but the way they answered the questions and the fact that their philosophies are all in line with what I'd like to see in a youth worker on our team. What about you, Alice?'

'I'm with you. They were the two standouts for me. The others were okay, but I didn't feel as connected with the three of them as much. Tilly and Jeremy were spot on.'

'Great.' Bec smiled.

'What do we do now?' Alice asked. 'This is my first interview panel.'

'Well, we've both made a decision. We won't offer the job until we call the third referee for both of them and then it has to go through human resources for a final check. If everything is in order, we should be able to make an offer to both of them tomorrow.'

'Fabulous. So, apart from our two new staff members, how's everything else going? With the camp, I mean.'

'In all the excitement last night, I had a brief talk with Chloe and Rosie after dinner. They didn't want to talk to me about it, but I asked how the buildings were going, and apparently, the bunkhouses are finished. The amenities block has to be tiled, but all the fittings are installed, and it's pretty much ready to go. So, we've still got a month up our sleeves, so we're good. I just have to wait for the funds to arrive and we can get the furniture sorted for the kitchen area, and we'll be ready. Building-wise anyway.'

'It's come together so quickly; I can't believe it.'

'Yes, it's been a pretty easy ride, this one. I'm looking forward to the camp. How many applicants for the camp do we have so far?' Bec asked.

'Well, now that we've reduced the age to ten, we've got quite a few from the primary schools in Augathella and Charleville, and the Catholic school as well. So, I think about fifteen applications for the juniors and from the high schools, I think we're up to about thirty. So, that'll give us forty-five, which I worry is too many.'

'Maybe, maybe not. We'll have to wait until we go out and have a look at the camp later in the week. If Jeremy and Tilly are successful, if they get through the rest of the process and they accept the positions, I'll leave it for a couple of days. I'd like to take them out and show them what we've done.'

'Sounds good to me.'

CHAPTER 13

Tilly

After meeting with Jeremy, Tilly tried to fill her afternoon and not focus on her churning emotions. She should have been on top of the world after the interview because she knew it had gone really well.

She didn't imagine many applicants would be prepared to travel west for a job that didn't pay terribly well, but it suited her.

She went to the World War II Centre, and as she walked around looking at the visual displays, she consciously pushed the thoughts of the conversation with Jeremy out of her mind. She couldn't cope with it this afternoon. Then later in the evening, after a solitary dinner at the hotel on the corner near the coffee shop, she went to the Cosmos Centre and tried to focus on the stars.

Accompanied by an interesting talk, what she saw through the telescopes was beyond all expectations, but she still couldn't get Jeremy Johnson out of her mind.

As soon as she saw him, all her feelings from ten years ago came flooding back. She couldn't believe it. She was a grown woman of almost thirty now. How could she still consider herself in love with someone she knew in her teens?

She lay back on the bed in the bland motel room and picked up her phone. It was eleven o'clock and she'd been up since dawn. She was hoping she'd get a call from Bec Hunter soon, one way or the other. If she was successful, she'd accept.

Jeremy had said he was going back to St. George, so she wouldn't have to worry about him being around. If she was unsuccessful, she'd drive up and see Nana, then head back to Brisbane, and look for a job. There was always plenty of bar and waitressing work, and hopefully, Chris would keep giving her a couple of days a week at the centre in the Valley.

Tilly hated not having a plan. Ever since she fled from Augathella, even though she'd had itinerant work and travelled to many destinations, she always had a plan ahead. Something to focus on, something to keep her thoughts in order.

Closing her eyes, she focused on her breathing and staying calm, putting into action some meditation techniques she'd learned over the years when she'd been feeling unhappy. She just got as far as relaxing her ankles, feet, toes, and up to her knees when her phone rang beside her. She grabbed it and pressed answer. 'Hello, Tilly Tingle speaking.'

'Hello Tilly, it's Bec Hunter here. How are you this morning?'

'I'm fine, thanks. How are you?'

'I'm really good. I'll get straight to it. It gives me great pleasure to offer you the position of youth worker for our community organisation, Choice For Youth.'

'Wow!' Tilly put a hand to her chest. 'That's wonderful, thank you so much.'

'Would you like a couple of hours to think about the offer after I outline the salary and the conditions attached to the full-time job?'

But Tilly shook her head, forgetting that Bec couldn't see her. 'No, no, no, that's fine, thank you. It also gives me great pleasure to say yes, I accept it.'

'That's fabulous,' Bec said. 'If you'd like to come into the office this afternoon, there are a few papers to sign. When you were here, you said you didn't have an address in Brisbane, but do you still have a job that you have to go back to?'

'No,' Tilly said. 'My casual work has ended

and I'm a free agent at the moment. So, whatever day suits you.'

'How about this afternoon?' Bec said.

'Could we make it tomorrow? Oh, hang on. No, this afternoon will be fine,' Tilly said quickly; she could drive up to Augathella tomorrow and see Nana.

'Are you sure?' Bec said.

'Yes, I was going to visit my grandmother in Augathella—not that you need to know all my personal stuff—to let her know that I was moving back to the district. I'm even hoping that I might live with her.'

'Who is your grandmother?' Bec asked curiously.

'Gladys Tingle.'

'Of course,' Bec said. 'It's an unusual name. I wondered if there was a relationship when we interviewed you.'

'Yes, I spent some of my childhood in

Augathella, but I haven't seen much of Nana since then, so I'm not sure whether she'll be in a position for me to move in with her. If not, I'll find somewhere else to live.'

'Well, if you need a hand with any of that, yell out and I'm happy to help.'

'Thank you. What time would you like me to come into the office? I can come in straight away if you like and then head off to Augathella.'

'That suits me perfectly. We can do it before I go to lunch,' Bec said.

'Thank you, Bec. Thank you so much. I'll see you soon.'

***

Bec

Bec had spoken to the referees for both of their chosen candidates. Both referees confirmed what Alice and Bec had picked up from interviews and resumes. Tilly Tingle had accepted the position and was coming in shortly.

Bec just had time to call Jeremy Johnson and offer him the other position. She dialled his number, and he picked up as quickly as Tilly had.

'Good morning, Jeremy, it's Bec Hunter here.'

'Good morning, Bec, good to hear from you.'

'Jeremy, we were very impressed yesterday, and we'd like to offer you the position as one of the youth workers at Choice for Youth in Charleville.'

'That's fabulous news, thank you so much.'

'Do you have any questions for me before you consider the position?'

'Just the hours and starting date, things like that.'

Bec quickly repeated what she told Tilly, offered the salary package and waited for Jeremy's reply.

'Would you like time to think about it?' she

said, 'Or can you give me a decision now? Not that I'm putting pressure on, but I've got a few other candidates I have to call.'

'Thanks so much for your call. I'm very happy to accept your offer. When would you like me to start?'

'What's your position? You still have a - you're still working at St. George Hospital?'

'But I'm only day-to-day casual. If you can just give me a couple of days to go back and sort out my stuff, I could start next week if that suits you.'

'That'll be great,' Bec said. 'Are you able to come in and sign some paperwork before you head back this afternoon?'

'I am. What time would you like me in?'

'Well, I have an appointment now, and then I'll take my lunch break. I hope it doesn't hold you up too much if I say about 1:30?'

'That's fine. I'll see you then, and thank you,

Bec. Great news. It will be good to be home.'

When the call ended, Bec quickly called the other three applicants, informing them that they were now on an eligibility list for any future positions because even if they weren't as good as the first two, they were excellent candidates.

Fifteen minutes later, she opened her email to find an acceptance of her funding grant and some paperwork to be filled out for the funding to go in. Bec sat back with her arms folded, satisfied that everything had gone so well. Life was pretty damn good.

CHAPTER 14

Tilly

Tilly stood at the door of her grandmother's house and knocked for the third time. Both the front and back doors were shut and locked, and all the windows were closed. She began to wonder if she'd gone away. Just as she was about to give up, the front gate creaked.

'Matilda! What are you doing here?' her grandmother asked with a stern face.

Tilly turned and smiled at her. 'Hello, Nana. I've come for a visit and a chat.'

'Well, you'd better come inside then. Just as well I baked yesterday.'

As usual, Nana was gruff, but the hug that she gave Tilly and the familiar smell of violet perfume made her feel welcome.

'It's so good to see you, Nana.' She hugged

her back as they stood on the front porch. 'I've got a job locally and I'm moving back to town.'

'Yes, but some might think you could've come back a little bit sooner than ten years, girl.'

Tilly nodded as guilt flooded through her. 'Yes, but I'm here now. Since you rang me about coming to stay a few months ago, I've given it a lot of thought, and well, here I am.'

Nana looked at her with a frown. 'Have you heard from your father lately?'

'Yes, he called me a couple of weeks ago. He's still at the Mt Isa mine.'

Tilly's mum passed away a couple of years after all the drama, and Tilly blamed the stress that her mother had endured for the fast onset of her illness. She would never forgive Jeremy's parents for that.

Mum's funeral had been in Dalby where she and Dad had spent most of their early married life, and where Tilly had attended primary school before the move to Augathella. Tilly had travelled from Brisbane to attend the funeral. Nana hadn't bothered coming; she'd never liked her daughter-in-law; that was the reason that Mum and Dad had moved to Dalby. After Mum's funeral, Dad based himself at Augathella as he took up fly-in fly-out work at various mines, and then a couple of years ago, he'd moved to Mt Isa, where he'd started a new relationship.

He hadn't been home to check on Nana since then, and it was Tilly's guilt that had brought her home.

'Barely rings me these days,' Nana complained. 'I might as well not have a son. Or a granddaughter.' She flicked a look at Tilly as she put the key in the front door.

'Well, the good news is, Nana, I've got a job in Charleville, and I was wondering whether you'd like me to come and live here with you.'

'Of course you can't. I won't be here much longer.'

'Oh, Nana!' Tilly panicked and grabbed her hand. 'Are you sick?'

'No, you silly girl, I've booked myself into the aged care facility. Got sick of caring for myself and cleaning a house. And waiting for you or your father to turn up.'

'Oh,' Tilly said slowly. 'I guess that's good news then. If you're happy about it.'

'Why wouldn't I be happy about it?' said Nana. 'All my friends are there, and Beryl's just moved in, so I'll have company instead of sitting here all day long waiting for my family to call me.'

'Well, I can come and visit you because I'll be living locally once I find somewhere to live.

'Don't think you're going to be staying here. I'm selling the house.'

'No. No, of course not. I'll find somewhere

to live. It would be easier for me to work and live in Charleville anyway because that's where I'll be working.'

'What's this job you've got?'

'I'm working with a youth centre in Charleville. It's called Choice For Youth.'

'Is that the one where Bec Hunter works?'

'Yes, it is.'

'She's a lovely girl. She looked after me when I was in hospital last year. I was at her engagement party last night.'

Tilly was surprised. 'Her engagement party? She didn't mention it. I did notice a pretty ring on her finger but I didn't realise it was new.'

'Yes, now there's a spirited girl for you; it was actually a surprise birthday party for her, and she proposed to her partner. He's a lovely young man, and they had a combined engagement party. Matt even asked me to dance.'

'She was very professional and kind,' Tilly

said.

'Rebecca was working at the hospital in the dementia ward for a while—but don't you go thinking that's why I was in there—and she had a bit to do with the aged care facility too. Rebecca told me that it would be worth my while going to the facility and having some company instead of wasting away lonely in this house.'

Tilly stifled a grin. If there was one thing that Nana wasn't in danger of, it was wasting away. Tilly had inherited her fine frame from her mother's side. The Tingles were all big-boned and broad-shouldered.

'That was kind of her to advise you. Are you sure you won't mind leaving your house?' Tilly asked as she followed Nana down the hall. The overpowering smell of mothballs that she always remembered surrounded her.

'Not one bit. I won't be locked up, though. I'm still free. I can come and go as I please. I can still do my committees and do the things around town where I'm very much needed.'

'I'm sure you are, Nana.'

'So where are you going to live, girl?'

'Don't worry. I'll rent in Charleville. Less driving.'

'Do you have enough money?'

'I have, Nana,' Tilly said with a smile.

'Good. And when are you starting work?'

'I'm not going back to Brisbane. I'm starting work tomorrow.'

'Well, you'd better find yourself somewhere to live.' A smile finally tilted Nana's lips. 'If you need to stay here, I can put you up for a couple of nights.'

'It's okay, Nana. I'll head back to Charleville soon and see what I can find. I'll come back and see you in a couple of days, though. Will you be here? When are you moving?'

158

'Not for a week or so. Now, would you like a cup of tea? I guess you're a bit grown up for the lemon syrup and fairy cakes you used to love.'

Nostalgia gripped Tilly. She and Dad used to come over to Nana's every Sunday when Mum was at church. She remembered the taste of the homemade lemon syrup cordial and fairy cakes well.

'Just a little bit grown up these days. And yes, a cup of tea would be good, thank you.' Tilly reached over and hugged Nana and was pleased when her grandmother clung to her for a few seconds.

Nana stepped back; her eyes were a bit misty. 'It is good to see you, Tilly.'

'It's good to be here with you too. I'm sorry it's been so long.' Tilly smiled, feeling the warmth come back to their relationship.

Nana relaxed, and they chatted happily until

Tilly left to return to Charleville. Now she had to find somewhere to live.

CHAPTER 15

Tilly checked into the Corones Hotel on her return to Charleville. She had decided to indulge herself with a nice room, a celebratory dinner, and a glass of wine. Her evening alone was pleasant, but as she sat in the outdoor area next to the restaurant, her thoughts inevitably turned to the days when she lived in Augathella, when she was still innocent, trusting, and happy.

The one thing Tilly could never move on from was her disappointment in Jeremy and how easily he had taken his parents' side. After the incident, he hadn't come to see her, and she left town the next day, much to her mother's distress.

It wasn't so much the accusation itself that made it difficult for Tilly to stay in town; it was primarily because Jeremy immediately believed the worst of her.

Over the past ten years, she had travelled the world, met countless people, and now realised that the incident in Augathella ten years ago wasn't as significant as she once thought. With maturity, she had gained perspective, but the disappointment in the young man she believed to be her soulmate always lingered.

When she saw Jeremy on the day of the interview, everything came rushing back. She managed to keep her composure, but she was overwhelmed by a surge of past emotions.

Some people believe in the concept of having a lifelong soulmate, the one you just know is the person for you when you first meet. Tilly might have been young, but she had believed Jeremy was her soulmate. They had been so close and made plans for the future together as they completed their final year of high school. Tilly was going to university to become a social worker, and Jeremy had applied for medical school. They had both chosen the same university in Brisbane and had spent many happy afternoons daydreaming about where they would live and the new life they would build together in the city.

But everything changed on that fateful afternoon. The afternoon she learned you couldn't trust anyone.

##

Tilly arrived at the youth centre on Thursday morning, excited to start work. Alice greeted her and immediately apologised. She was ill and Bec was out of town at a conference.

'I'm so sorry, Tilly. I'm not feeling well, so I'm going to take the next two days off. Maybe you could start on Monday instead?'

Tilly was disappointed. 'I'm happy to manage the office today. I can take messages, do filing, or do anything you can give me. If that suits you and Bec, of course.'

'That would be awesome. Bec asked me to apologise for her having to go away at short notice. I haven't been able to reach her this morning to let her know I'm not well. If you're fine with doing some data entry, organising files, and reading our policy documents, that would be great. The only thing is you'll be in the office by yourself.'

'That's not a problem,' Tilly replied.

Alice covered her mouth with her forearm and coughed. 'It's not COVID. I did a test this morning. I just have a head cold from getting wet in the rain last week,' Alice explained as she led Tilly into the office.

Tilly had been in the reception area during her interview and was pleasantly surprised as she looked around the airy office space. A large window overlooked a flat grass area with a barbeque table and outdoor seating.

'That's the outdoor area.' Alice gestured to

the window. 'We hold a lot of youth meetings and functions outside. The council provided the barbeque and outdoor furniture. It's a popular area with the kids—a few of them don't like being confined—and we also have our breaks out there. That's Bec's desk over there. She has the humongous screen, but if you'd like to use it today, feel free. My desk is over in the corner, and there are three other workstations with computers, so pick whichever one you like, make it yours and settle in. Again, I'm sorry that you're going to be here alone today.'

'No problem at all. Just show me quickly what I need to do, and I'll settle in.'

Alice walked over to a bank of filing cabinets adjacent to the entrance and pointed to the one on the left. 'In the top drawer here, you'll see policy documents. They're all clearly marked. Pull out the ones on our mission statement and the philosophy of the centre, and read about what Choice for Youth is about. It's a great initiative, and we've been fortunate that Bec is an excellent grants person. She knows how to secure funding. She was really happy yesterday when we received confirmation that the grant she applied for—for the Easter camp—at the lake came through.' Alice pointed to a pile of folders on the last desk. 'The applications for the camp need to be sorted too, by age groups and gender. As soon as we're back in the office on Monday and the other new youth worker arrives, we'll really get into organising the camp. I know Bec wants us all to go out and look at the site.'

'It sounds great. I'm so happy to be here,' Tilly said.

'And we're happy to have you. I think you'll fit in really well.' Alice turned away and held her breath, then let out a loud sneeze. 'I'm so sorry, I'm going to have to get out of here. I'll leave you my mobile number in case you have any questions. You probably have Bec's number on your phone, but don't call her today because she's on a course over in Roma.'

'That's a fair drive, isn't it?'

'Yeah, she left early this morning, and she'll be back late tomorrow night, so we'll both see you on Monday morning. If you're able to come in a little bit early, maybe an eight o'clock start instead of nine like today, that would be good. We're pretty flexible with hours, but the system is fair.'

'Sounds good to me,' Tilly said.

'Thank you so much.'

When Alice left, Tilly locked the main door and settled into the tasks that Alice had given her.

The first two days in the office gave Tilly an opportunity to learn what they were doing, and she was really impressed. She was also excited to be a part of the team, and as Alice had said, it seemed that Bec was a whiz at getting funding. She read the write-up on the Easter camp, and it sounded really good. It was being held at the property near the Calthorpe's place, and when Tilly recognised Kimberley's married name, she realised Kimberley must live out that way now. If she got a chance over the weekend, she would give her a call and organise a catchup.

According to Nana, a few people she went to school with still lived in Augathella. Excluding Jeremy, of course; she preferred not to think about him at the moment.

Tilly spent her second day in the office looking at the camp applications. Some of the names from all those years ago were familiar: Cartwright, Mason, Wilson—all names she knew from high school. She wondered how much the rumour had spread through town ten years ago and whether her reputation had been tainted by lies.

For the second time since she arrived, her thoughts took her back to that day.

Mum had begged her to stay as Tilly packed her bags. 'Sweetheart, people who knew you won't believe the Johnsons.'

Anyway, that was water under the bridge now, and yes, Mum had probably been right. In hindsight, she knew her friends wouldn't have judged her on what had happened, or more to the point, what had been said, but at the time, all she wanted to do was get away.

As her mother had said to her at the time: 'Those who know you and love you know that it's a lie. And anyone else who thinks the worst of you, that's their problem.'

It had taken Tilly quite a few years to accept that, but she had moved on now. Now she was back in town, and she was here to stay as long as the job lasted. When she caught up with

Kimberley she would tell her why she'd left so suddenly.

Tilly finished all the tasks Alice had given her on Friday afternoon around three o'clock and locked the door with a smile as she left the youth centre. She had made the right decision; the work here was going to be fulfilling.

She had always wanted to continue her education, and now that she had her Certificate in Youth Work, she was motivated to research a university course. She had the time to study now and a job where she could put the theory into practice. Things had certainly taken a turn for the better. It might have taken ten years, but Tilly had finally settled somewhere. She had come full circle, back to the area where she had spent her happiest years.

CHAPTER 16

Kimberley

When her phone rang after dinner on Friday night, Kimberley was pleased to hear Tilly's voice and even happier when she heard her good news.

'I got the job, Kim. I've already started work, and I love it,' Tilly said. 'Thanks so much for your reference supporting me.'

'My pleasure, Tilly, but your qualifications and experience would have held equal weight.'

'Now that I'm back to stay, let's catch up.'

Kimberley smiled at the happiness in Tilly's voice. 'I'd love to. It's fabulous that you're back home. When are you free?'

'Whenever it suits you. I can come up to Augathella any time.'

'How about tomorrow morning? I've got a

meeting at Jenna's Tearoom at lunchtime, but I could get there earlier. Are you sure you're happy to drive up?'

'Yes, I'll take the opportunity to see Nana too. You give me a time, and I'll be there. That's the tearoom on the highway, isn't it?'

'That's right. Is ten o'clock too early for you?'

'That's fine. I'll see you then. And Kim?'

'Yes?'

'I've got a lot to tell you. About why I left and everything.'

'It will be good to catch up. I'll see you tomorrow.'

Kimberley was thoughtful as she hung up. Quinn was engrossed in the football on the television in the living room, so she sat down in the study, opened up an old photo album, and let nostalgia take hold as she flicked through the photos of their last year at high school.

They'd been a tight group; she and Tilly and Sophie Cartwright had been close friends. Tilly had been madly in love with Jeremy Johnson, Kimberley had always had a crush on Quinn, who was a couple of years ahead of them, and Sophie Cartwright and Kent Mason had been a couple. That year had been so much fun; they'd all managed to socialise around study and final exams, but suddenly everything had changed when the exams were over. Many of them had moved on pretty much straight away. Kimberley had left for university in January, but Tilly had left town suddenly the weekend after the last exam in mid-December. Kimberley had been hurt that she had left without saying goodbye, but her plans had soon taken over.

It would be good to have Tilly back in town. They had been good friends and she'd always regretted losing touch.

Kimberley stared at a photo of Jeremy and

Tilly at the Year Twelve formal.

She hadn't heard anything back from Jeremy since she agreed to be his referee, and she wondered if he'd been successful as well. Tilly hadn't mentioned Jeremy, but Kimberley wasn't sure what that meant. She'd be careful what she said when they met in the morning.

##

Kimberley walked into the tea room mid-morning on Saturday. There were no empty tables, and she wondered if Jenny Riley had remembered to book a table for their lunch meeting. Jenny had seemed distracted lately.

Since Jenna renovated dear old Reg's house and opened the tearooms, it had become a popular meeting place for locals and a popular highway stop for tourists and grey nomads travelling along the Matilda Highway.

Kimberley smiled as she spotted Tilly sitting at a table on the side verandah. When Kimberley walked over, Tilly stood and held her arms open, and they shared a big hug.

'Oh my goodness, Tils, it's so good to see you. It's been such a long time, and you know what? You don't look any different.'

'Neither do you, Kim.'

'I wish,' she said. 'I feel like I've aged twenty years since I took on the assistant principal role this year.'

'You look fine. How long have you been back in town?' Tilly asked as they sat opposite each other.

'I came back a couple of years after I finished my teaching degree. I did some casual work in Brisbane, but I've been back here over six years now.'

They sat at the table and waited for their order to be taken. Tilly looked at her and said, 'How long have you and Quinn been married?'

'Six months. We didn't want the whole

shebang and the cost that goes with it, so we eloped. We were home about three weeks before anyone twigged, and then we had a quiet dinner at the pub with our closest friends.'

'And are you happy living on the farm out of town?'

'How did you know we're out on the property?'

Tilly smiled. 'I knew that Quinn's family had land out there. It's all you used to talk about. I was so pleased to hear you ended up together. But to answer your question, Alice Templeton at Choice for Youth told me that the Easter camp is out there near your farm. I didn't know there was a campsite out there.'

Kimberley frowned. 'There have been some big changes in the district over the past six months. We've got these generous new people in town who are injecting so much money into different projects. Remember the lake we camped at for our Year 12 retreat? They've built a proper camp there.'

Kimberley watched as Tilly's expression changed.

'That lake? I didn't know that's where the Easter camp was being held. I don't remember that camp being near Quinn's place.'

Kimberley nodded. 'It was. Don't you remember how much I was hoping that Quinn would turn up even though he wasn't in our year? I thought at the time he might because the camp was close to their farm. And I was so disappointed when he didn't come.'

'I'm sorry.' Tilly shook her head. 'I don't remember that.'

Kimberley almost commented that Tilly had been too wrapped up in Jeremy to notice much back then, but she held the words back.

'I went over and had a look last night. The buildings are rustic inside, with an American redwood forest-type look, and the outdoor areas are fantastic. But you'll see it when you're out there at camp.'

'I think we're going out there to have a look next week.'

'It's fantastic, Tilly. Wait till you see it.'

'Hi, ladies, are you ready to order?'

Kimberley looked up at Ellie as she waited with pen poised. 'I'll have a flat white, thanks. Tilly, how about you?'

'I'll have the same, thank you.'

'Ellie, do you know if Jenny Riley booked the table for lunch?'

'Table's booked for eleven. Amelia rang up yesterday.'

'Great. Jenna's not around today?

'No, she and Joshua have gone out somewhere for the day. I'm the boss.'

'You're a good girl, Ellie,' Kimberley said. 'Even though it makes me feel old seeing you working.' She grinned at Tilly as Ellie chuckled and hurried back to the counter. 'I do feel old. That's Ellie Wilson, Craig and Lorraine's daughter. She was in Year Six at the school when I started there. Now she's finished high school and working.'

'Time goes quickly,' Tilly agreed.

Kimberley sat back as they waited for their coffees. 'Tell me what you've been up to, Tilly. We lost touch when you left town so quickly after we finished our exams, and then I didn't know where to get in touch with you.'

Tilly stared at her; her mouth set in a straight line.

'Then your mum and dad left soon after, and we had no forwarding address and no way to contact you.'

Tilly spoke slowly. 'It was a difficult time for me, Kim.'

'What happened to you and Jeremy? I

thought you guys were made for each other. You always used to talk about each other being your soulmates.'

'I thought that too, but when it came to the crunch, he didn't support me.'

'What do you mean came to the crunch? You weren't pregnant, were you?' she asked.

'Oh, God no, Mum and Dad would've killed me if I'd been pregnant at eighteen.'

'Are you able to tell me what happened, or is it private?'

'I know you won't judge me, Kimberley, because you knew me well enough. I should have told you back then, but I was so upset, I wasn't thinking straight.'

'Upset? What happened?'

'It was a hard time. Remember how I was working for Jeremy's parents on weekends, out at that store on the road to Wardville?'

'Yes, I do. The general store just on the edge

of town.'

'Well, I worked all day the Saturday after my last exam. Remember that day? The boys were all at the pub, celebrating being eighteen and the exams being over. By the time I finished work, Jeremy had gone home and had an early night, and I didn't see him.'

'I do remember that. Some of the girls were there for a couple of hours, and I remember you were at work. Old Sarge made sure none of the boys drove home.'

'I went to work on Sunday morning to do the morning shift. The Johnsons stayed open for the Sunday papers when they came in on the plane, and then we closed at lunchtime. I was there by myself for a couple of hours because Mrs Johnson wasn't feeling well, and Mr Johnson never worked on a Sunday.' She put her head down and looked at her hands folded in her lap. 'He came in that day. And that's when it happened.'

'What? What happened?' Kimberley asked.

Tilly paused as Ellie brought the coffee to the table. She stared past Kimberley and gave a brief nod as her coffee was placed on the table. When Ellie had walked away, Tilly continued, her voice flat and expressionless. 'I'd always felt uncomfortable around Jeremy's dad. He used to like to stand close to me and was a bit touchy when there was no one else there. When Mrs Johnson or Jeremy were there, he barely acknowledged me. So he came in mid-morning on that Sunday, and he actually . . .'

'He actually what?' Kimberley asked.

'He put his hand on my breast,' she said.

'What? What did you do?' Kimberley widened her eyes. 'Oh Tilly, that's awful.'

Tilly's lips lifted in a slight smile. 'I kneed him in the place that it hurts and told him to never touch me again.'

'Good on you, girl. And who did you tell? Did you report it? What did Jeremy say?'

'That's the problem,' she said. 'I knew no one would believe me, so I just didn't say anything.'

'But that's assault. Sexual assault.'

'Well, I suppose I assaulted him back. When I kneed him, he doubled up, but he told me not to say anything or he'd make sure I was sorry.'

'I can believe that. He always was a hard man. I remember.'

'Jeremy had issues with him too. They used to fight a lot, but I never got involved, and I never said anything.'

'So what happened? Why did you leave town? Were you embarrassed?'

'No, I went in on Monday morning, and Mrs Johnson accused me of stealing a thousand dollars from the till when I was there by myself the day before.'

'What? I don't believe a word of it.'

'She told me that they'd already contacted Sarge and that the word was around town. I was mortified. I'm surprised you didn't hear about it. I'm sure they bad-mouthed me after I left. Even Dad sat me down and told me to tell them the truth and asked what I wanted the money for! That was the breaking point for me. I left Augathella, and I was on a Greyhound bus to Brisbane the next day.'

'Oh, Tilly, really? You should have come to me.'

Tilly lifted her head, and her eyes were sad. 'And you know the worst part of all? Jeremy believed them, and he didn't even come to see me. He totally wiped me. And the first time I've seen him since then was when I ran into him in Charleville this week.'

'Oh, sweetie, are you okay?'

Tilly shook her head and her eyes filled with

tears. 'You know what, Kim? I've spent the last ten years convincing myself that I was over Jeremy. I've tried to have other relationships, but every time I think I'm getting close to a guy, it feels wrong. No matter what Jeremy did, and not matter that he didn't trust me or come to see if I was all right, I've spent ten years still hoping that he still loves me. It was as though we were connected. He was my soulmate, and no one else has ever come close.'

CHAPTER 17

Matt was already up and working when Bec woke up. The trip to Roma, the two intensive days of professional development, and then the long drive home last night had been exhausting. She was surprised to see it was almost ten when she woke up. She quickly jumped in the shower, then dried her hair, found an ironed dress in the wardrobe, and applied a coat of lip gloss.

'Good morning, sleepyhead.' Matt looked up from his computer as she came into the kitchen. He was at the table surrounded by piles of paper and two shoeboxes overflowing with receipts.

'Craig Wilson?' she asked with a sympathetic smile after she kissed him.

'Yep. I'll be here all day.'

'Do you mind if I go to Jenna's for this meeting?' she asked. 'Or is there something I can help you with?'

'Thanks, sweetheart, but no. I really need to finish this return for him today. He gave me his receipts and things a bit late,' Matt replied. 'I feel bad because we haven't seen each other for a couple of days, and I'll be here most of the day.'

'All good. I've got a masquerade ball planning meeting at Jenna's at eleven, and I need to get some groceries first, not to mention the huge pile of washing to tackle when I get home. I'll only be gone for an hour or two,' she assured him. 'I'll bring you some lunch home.'

'Another ball meeting? Didn't you have one a couple of weeks ago?'

'We did, but Jenny Riley called a few days ago because she wants to hand over the reins to someone else.'

'That's unusual for Jenny. She's usually the

one leading these events,' Matt commented. 'What's the ball for anyway? And why is it being organised so early?'

'Jenny has had some great ideas, and starting early means a good lead time for everything, but I am a bit worried about her.'

'I was talking to her at the supermarket the other day, and she didn't seem like her usual bubbly self,' Matt said. 'I hope she's okay.'

Bec leaned over and kissed him again. 'I'll suss her out, and I'll see you later. Let's have a nice dinner tonight and spend some time together. Do you think you'll be finished with Craig's BAS by then?'

'I can only hope,' Matt replied. 'Have fun and say hello to everyone for me.'

'What would you like me to bring home from Jenna's?'

'A hamburger? With the works?'

'Will do. See you in a while.'

A few minutes later, Bec parked at the side of Jenna's Vintage Tearoom. As usual, the car park was jammed with caravans and motorhomes, but when Bec parked, she recognised a few of the local cars. As she locked the car, a small sedan passed her, and she recognised Tilly Tingle. By the time she realised it was Tilly, it was too late to wave. Alice had told her last night that Tilly had been in to work for the last two days.

Bec ran lightly up the stairs and glanced across to the shaded veranda. A dozen local women were already sitting at the table drinking coffee.

'Hi, Bec.' Kimberley waved her over. 'Sit here next to me. How's your week been?'

Bec sat on the vacant chair beside Kimberely and smiled. 'Busy. Interviews and a two-day course in Roma. How about you?'

'Really good, busy as usual at school.'

'How did you go with the interviews? I know Tilly's already started. I just had coffee with her.'

'I thought it was Tilly driving out when I got out of the car.'

'Am I allowed to ask who got the other position?' Kimberley asked.

'Sure, not a problem at all. Both have been signed up, and the unsuccessful candidates have been advised and put on the eligibility list. You'll be pleased to hear both your friends you gave references for have been appointed.'

Kimberley frowned and answered slowly. 'Oh. I guess Jeremy will be pleased too.'

'You've all been friends for a long time, obviously?'

'Yes, you could say that. We were all in the same year at school. Bec, look, I hope I'm not speaking out of turn, but keep an eye on Tilly. When she rang to ask me about being her referee, she asked me if Jeremy still lived in town. I don't think she knew he was going for the job too.'

'Okay, thanks for the heads up.'

'I won't breach any confidences, but as long as they get on, that's the main thing.'

Bec nodded and wondered if she'd made a mistake. Everything was going so well, and she hoped there wouldn't be a conflict between her two new youth workers.

Amelia stood at the end of the table and hit her cup with a spoon. 'Everyone ready to order?' she called out over the loud buzz of conversation.

Bec stood and Amelia's attention. 'Amelia, I'll go over and tell Ellie we're ready to order.'

'Thanks, Bec. We'll talk while we eat. I need to get home early because Ben has to go out to Charleville when I get home.' Amelia blinked as she held Bec's gaze.

Something wasn't right.

Kimberley turned to Bec as she moved to the counter. 'Bec, have you got time to have a bit of a talk after the meeting?'

'I do. What's up?' Bec looked at Kimberley curiously.

'I'll tell you later,' Kimberley whispered.

CHAPTER 18

Ellie had been too busy to come to the table to take their orders, so Amelia had marked them in pencil on one of the laminated menus.

As she waited at the counter, Bec walked over.

'How are you, Amelia? Is Jenny okay?'

'I'm good, but Jenny had to go to the hospital with Tom.'

'Oh, I hope everything is okay.'

'Well, not exactly, but keep it between you and Matt. Tom's going to have some tests to see if he needs to see a specialist in Brisbane.'

'Oh, I'm so sorry to hear that. Tom's a lovely guy.'

'Yes, he is. I'm worried about Jenny, she's not coping well at all.'

'Jenny was really looking forward to organising the ball, but Tom's health certainly takes priority. I'll keep an eye out for her.' Bec reached over and touched Amelia's hand. 'And you and Ben too. That's what friends are for.'

The meals were out in twenty minutes, and Amelia stood and waited for the girls to stop chatting.

'First, we've set the date of the ball. It's the last Saturday in August, and it will be called the Spring Ball. Is everyone happy with that?'

Nods around the table confirmed that there was no disagreement, so Amelia continued.

'We've talked to Harry at the hospital, and they're delighted that the hospital is going to be the major fundraising recipient. Most of the funds raised will go to the maternity wing. It's fantastic to see the wing open again, but Harry indicated it will take more funding to keep it open.'

Callie spoke up. 'I agree. It's great that all the new mums don't have to travel to Charleville, and with all the new young couples in town, there will be even more of a need.'

'Okay,' Amelia said. 'Jenny's asked me to get some creative ideas for the ball from all of you today . . . for a theme. What does everyone think? Should we have a theme, or what's the best way to go about it?'

The silence at the table lasted for a while as they all thought and then Callie, Sophie and Rosie started to speak at once. There were some chuckles, and Callie and Sophie sat back, and indicated for Rosie to talk.

'Go ahead, Rosie,' Callie said. 'We love your ideas.'

Rosie's eyes lit up. 'Well, before we moved to Australia—I know it's very different because of our history over in the UK—but we had a Masquerade Ball in the village hall, and it raised a lot of money for our local community. Our masquerade had a sort of theme with costumes from the last century and everyone had to wear a face mask.'

Bec looked across the table as Gladys Tingle gave a disapproving grunt. She smiled at Rosie and nodded, encouraging her to go on.

Rosie spoke quickly. 'The best thing was that we held craft afternoons in the weeks leading up to it, and we all got together and made different masks. Then the masks were all swapped around, sort of drawn out of a hat, so no one knew who got what mask.'

Amelia smiled. 'I like that idea. What does everyone else think, Callie, what about you?'

Callie Cartwright leaned forward. 'I think it's a great idea, but instead of having a British historical theme, why don't we have an early "set in Australia" theme and we could have all different masks?'

Sophie Mason got on board. 'We could even have masks of Australian animals and birds to match our dresses.'

'I love the idea,' Bec said. 'What do you think, Amelia?'

Amelia nodded. 'I think it sounds fabulous, and I think with Jenny being so crafty, she'd love to take it over. She should be back on deck next week . . . we hope.'

There was a bit of an awkward silence. Everyone wondered what was wrong, but no one asked—not even Gladys.

Amelia continued. 'So, will we assign some committee roles? Jenny is the chair of the committee. I suppose we should take some notes about this.'

Sophie whipped out her phone, 'I'm happy to take the notes as secretary. I can record it here and email it to you all later when I check it.'

'Great, we have a secretary,' Chloe said. 'Do we need a treasurer?'

'Probably not just yet,' Amelia said. 'But

once we get closer, we might need to look at how we're going to raise extra funds on the night.'

Gladys Tingle hadn't spoken since she'd given her disapproving snort and Bec tensed as she spoke.

'Perhaps we could have a raffle and sell some tickets in town. We could make some crocheted rugs and doilies. And maybe Jenna would be happy to sell the tickets at the counter here?'

Bec's shoulders relaxed. 'Great idea, Gladys.'

'The problem is, with raffles, we do need one valuable prize,' Sophie chimed in.

'I think a raffle sounds like a great idea,' Amelia said. 'We need to get someone to approach the local businesses and see if we can get some donations.'

Chloe put her hand up. 'I'm happy to do that, but let's ask statewide too. The better the first prize, the more tickets we'll sell. We've got plenty of time.'

'Seven months,' Gladys said.

Sophie nodded. 'Good idea, Chloe. I'm happy to write to a heap of businesses. Bec, I know you're busy with the youth centre at the moment, but would you be happy to help me? You're such a good grant writer. Maybe we could get together and write some letters to some of the bigger corporations, maybe get holiday prizes and things like that.'

'Sounds good to me,' Bec said. 'Yes, I'm happy to help you.'

The conversations went on for another half hour, and Amelia finally sat back with a smile. 'I think Jenny's going to be very pleased with that. So did you get all that down?' she asked Sophie.

'Noted it all, I'll type it up when I get home. I think I've got just about everybody's email here except for Gladys and Beryl.'

Gladys shook her head. 'I don't have one, but maybe Tilly does? She could print it out for me.'

'Me either,' Beryl added.

'That sounds like a plan,' Sophie said. 'I'll get the minutes to you both somehow, even if I print them and drop them in.'

'One copy will do,' Gladys said. 'We'll have the same address from next week when I move into the facility.'

'Shall we set the date for the next meeting?' Amelia asked. 'How about four weeks from today?'

'Sounds good.' There was a lot of nodding as Ellie came over to clear away the lunch dishes.

With calls of 'goodbye' and 'see you soon', the group broke up and headed down the stairs and out to their cars. Bec waited for Amelia to come down the stairs. When she'd been working at the hospital, she and Matt had had a couple of weekends away camping with Ben and Amelia.

Amelia caught up to her in the car park.

'Are you okay, Amelia?'

'Yeah, I'm coping. Just dreading going home to Ben and finding out what the verdict is today.'

'So Tom's test results will be back straight away?'

'Sort of. I think we all know that something is wrong. He's becoming very forgetful, and he's losing track of time. Jenny suspects he's in the early stages of dementia. Ben's not coping well.'

'Oh no, Tom's young.'

'Yes, apparently, it can impact people of all ages. Tom's only fifty-nine.'

'Thanks for taking over. I was getting a bit choked up there.'

'I saw that, and that's what friends are for.'

Bec hugged Amelia as her eyes filled with tears. 'You and Ben know where to find us.

Come around anytime you need a break or just need to talk.'

'Thanks, Bec. We will.'

CHAPTER 19

Bec - Jenna's Vintage Tearoom

'I'll have to be quick, Kim. I told Matt I wouldn't be long, and I've got a stack to do this afternoon.'

'Me too. Quinn's waiting for me to get home. We're going out this afternoon with the trailer to get some firewood in. It's going to be cold soon.'

"What's wrong?' Bec asked as they walked down to the car park. It had emptied out as the lunch crowd had gone, and the only ones left were Gladys and Beryl. Gladys was helping Beryl put her walker in the back of the small car.

'I've been thinking more about Jeremy and Tilly and what I told you. I'm going to catch up with Jeremy as soon as I can and see where he is.'

'What do you mean? Where he is?'

'Where he is in terms of his relationship with Tilly. They were a very tight couple, and I know Tilly still has feelings. If Jeremy is still interested, I am going to play matchmaker. Do you want to help me?'

Bec smiled. 'I think they would make a lovely couple.'

'They did,' Kimberley said sadly. 'But something happened. I won't share it with you, as Tilly told me in confidence, but I'm determined to suss Jeremy out.'

***

'Jeremy, it's Kim here, Kimberley Calthorpe. I believe congratulations are in order.' Kimberley lifted her shoulder and tucked the phone to her ear as she wiped down the kitchen countertop after lunch on Sunday afternoon. She'd given a lot of thought to what Tilly had said.

'Hi Kim, how are you?'

'I'm good.'

'Thank you so much for the reference. I'm assuming it was a pretty good one because I got one of the jobs at Choice for Youth.'

'Yes, I asked Bec when we were at a meeting yesterday. I hope you don't mind the news being out there already. It's probably right around town by now.'

'No, that's fine. I'm looking forward to starting.'

'When do you start?' she asked.

'Tomorrow morning. I nipped back to St George on Friday, and I'm just unpacking at the flat I've rented in Charleville.'

'We're having a barbeque tonight. It might be too far for you to drive, but we'd love you to come. There'll be a few of our friends from school here.'

Jeremy was quiet for a moment. 'Will Tilly be there?' he asked.

'Tilly Tingle? No, she won't. Just a few couples. I'm sure you remember Kent Mason, and Quinn, of course. Everyone wants to catch up with you. Would you have time to drive up? It won't be a late night. We'll kick off around four o'clock.'

'That would be great, thank you.'

'Excellent.' Kimberley quickly gave Jeremy the road address of their farm, so he could put it into his GPS.

'I'll see you around four. What can I bring?'

'Just yourself.'

As soon as she disconnected, Kimberley called the Ingrams, the Masons, and Bec and Matt.

Maybe seeing happy couples might get him thinking.

For only a brief moment, Kimberley wondered if she was doing the right thing. Then she remembered Tilly's eyes brimming with tears, and she knew she was.

She filled Quinn in when he came in from the shed. 'We're having a barbie tonight, love. Jeremy Johnson's coming too.'

He raised his eyebrows. 'Am I suspecting an ulterior motive in this? It's not like you to organise a barbecue on such short notice.'

'Yes, I need to get to the bottom of something before tomorrow.'

'Bottom of what?' her husband asked.

'Well, remember Jeremy Johnson?'

'Yes,' he said.

'And Tilly Tingle?'

'Yes, I remember them both.'

'Well, we haven't seen them for ten years, and they're both starting work together at the Youth Centre in Charleville tomorrow.'

'And?' Quinn's eyebrows rose again.

'And I've got a feeling that this needs a little bit of investigation tonight.'

Quinn stared at Kimberley as she filled the kettle. 'You're not treading on toes, are you, Kim?'

'No, it's something I feel strongly about. I've had a good talk with Tilly, and I think this is something I need to do. I need to talk to Jeremy and find out whether he knows she's starting work with him tomorrow and then suss out his feelings. Both of them are still single. Doesn't that tell you something?'

'It tells me they've been busy.' Quinn grinned at her.

'I'll give you busy,' she said. 'How about you go out and get the firepit sorted, and I'll bring a cuppa out to you?'

At four o'clock, the fire was well alight, and the kitchen bench was covered with bowls of salad and the meat that Quinn had brought over from the big refrigerator in the shed.

Kent and Sophie were the first to arrive with baby Rosie, followed by Bec and Matt. Fallon and John arrived soon after with little Ryan, and soon they were sitting around the fire chatting. The sound of a car pulling into the driveway caught Kim's attention, and she jumped up.

'That must be Jeremy now. I'll go and meet him.'

She took off before anyone could come with her. She wanted to have Jeremy to herself for a while and find out what she needed to know.

CHAPTER 20

Tilly

Because Nana was busy at a meeting on Saturday, Tilly went back to Charleville after she had coffee with Kimberley and called into one of the real estate offices. She was disappointed to find out that there was very little available to rent.

'Check with Bec Hunter,' the receptionist said. 'I think Damien, our property manager, told her about a couple of flats available when she was asking last week.'

'I will, thank you.'

Tilly frowned as she headed back to the hotel. Perhaps she could stay in the hotel over the weekend and talk to Bec on Monday to see if she had any suggestions. And if the worst came to worst, there was always Augathella. Surely there would be something up there. So, having had no luck, she settled into her hotel room and had a relaxing weekend. She tried to push any thoughts of Jeremy Johnson from her mind and was successful—for some of the time.

On Monday morning, at 7:45 a.m., Tilly unlocked and pushed open the door of the Choice for Youth Centre.

Even after two days at the hotel, she felt at home in the office. Maybe it was because she had been there by herself and hadn't had to share the office with anybody. But she felt comfortable there. Today would be different, but she was still looking forward to the work ahead.

She crossed to the desk she'd chosen, opened the drawer, and put her car keys in there. When she turned around, Bec was walking through the door.

'Welcome, Tilly. An official hello.' Bec

smiled at her. 'I'm so sorry you were here by yourself on Thursday and Friday. Poor Alice is still a bit shaky on it. She said she was going to try and come in today, but she still doesn't feel well enough. She assures me it's not COVID, she just has a head cold.'

'I was fine,' Tilly said. 'It gave me a good chance to read everything and get to know a bit about the place. With the centre up and running only a couple of months, you've certainly got a lot done.'

'Yeah, it's been good. I'm really enjoying it. Bit different from my last job. I did love that one too, but it just got too hard after a while.'

'You worked at the hospital in the dementia wing, didn't you? My grandmother mentioned it.'

'Yes, I did. I did love the oldies, but I used to take a lot of the worry home with me. Especially those whose families weren't a bit interested in coming to see them. They were so lonely, it broke my heart.'

'Not that youth work is any easier,' Tilly said. 'A lot of the time in Brisbane, I think if I'd had a bigger home, I would've ended up fostering a few kids. Some people should never have children. A lot of them do it hard, and we had so many homeless kids that we ran a soup kitchen there three days a week, and we were always full.'

'Yes, I'm already worrying about some of the kids who come here. You'll meet them this afternoon. I forgot to mention that we're having a welcome afternoon to greet you and Jeremy.'

Tilly froze and stared at Bec. 'Jeremy?'

'The other new youth worker. I'm sorry I thought you knew, but then of course, Alice wasn't here, so she wouldn't have told you.'

'Oh. What's his last name?' she asked casually.

'Johnson. He starts this morning.'

'Jeremy Johnson,' Tilly repeated.

That's why he was in town on Wednesday.

Thoughts were running furiously through her mind. He had been in town on Wednesday, but he said he was there for an appointment. He didn't say an interview. And as far as she knew, he was a nurse. Surely, he hadn't retrained as a youth worker.

But he must have.

Oh, God, how was she going to cope with working with him?

Bec was looking at her curiously. 'Is there a problem?'

'No, no, just coincidental. I bumped into Jeremy in town on the day of the interviews. We were friends at high school.'

Friends? Not really the right word for the relationship they'd had in their teens.

Her hands were shaking, and her mouth was dry. She resisted giving any indication that there was a problem with working with Jeremy. She didn't want to jeopardise this job, so she would talk to him and deal with it.

She forced a chuckle. 'Well, what a coincidence. We've both come back to the region. And we both trained as youth workers. We haven't seen each other for years.' Her voice was flippant as she hid the turmoil within. She tried to change the subject.

'Oh, Bec. While I think of it, I went to the real estate agency to find somewhere to live, and they suggested you might know of a flat.'

Tilly frowned as a strange expression crossed Bec's face.

'I do,' she said. 'The shire asked the agency to put aside two flats in case some of the new staff needed something. I'll show you later.'

'Thank you, sounds good.'

'Okay,' Bec said, 'Come and I'll show you what we're doing today. As soon as we get Jeremy through the orientation process, we'll go out to the campsite; it shouldn't take too long. You're probably an expert, considering you did your own on Thursday and Friday.'

Tilly smiled back, finally starting to calm down a little. 'Honestly, I didn't mind. It was a good introduction to get to know the place.'

'Well, once we've taken him through that and given him his key and everything, we're going to go down to the council and have a look at a couple of buses that they've got. It all depends on how many kids we decide on. Did you have a look at the applications that Alice left?'

'Yes, I did. I did recognise a lot of the names from school.'

'Some are new to Augathella too,' Bec said. 'Our main goal today is to go out to the campsite.

The generous benefactors who are letting us stay at the retreat, I might add for no charge, are Chloe and Rosie, who I'm sure you'll meet if you spend some time in Augathella. Anyway, they rang me over the weekend to say that the buildings are all finished.'

'Is that quicker than you expected,' Tilly asked.

'It was a big shock, I can't believe it. They only bought the land a couple of months ago, and not only did they have to go through the appropriate paperwork and permissions and get everything approved by the council, but they also had to find a builder to build the bunkhouses, an amenities block and a cookhouse.'

'That is fast. I can't wait to see it.'

'We need to look at the layout before we decide how many kids are going to come. Once we take a look, we can come back and get this camp organised.'

'Sounds good to me. So, it's only you, Alice, Jeremy, and I for the camp,' Bec said. 'We really need to look at numbers. We do have some volunteers from Augathella—two or three couples who are going to come out and do some of the activities and help with the cooking. My only worry is that they won't have as much time as they think because Easter is big in Augathella.'

'I remember,' Tilly said. 'The billy cart derby, the rodeo, and the races. It was a lot of fun when we were in high school.' Her head flew up as the door opened, and Jeremy walked in, his eyes wide when he saw her standing there.

'Tilly!' he said, his brows drawing together in a frown.

'Jeremy!' she said, taking total control of her emotions. 'What a coincidence. Both of us starting the same jobs in Charleville.'

Bec stepped forward with a wide smile. 'I

believe there are no introductions needed. Tilly tells me that you both know each other from high school.'

'We did,' Jeremy said, his voice wary. 'We knew each other quite well at school, didn't we, Tilly?'

'Yes, we did, Jeremy,' she said.

'Fabulous,' Bec said. 'Tilly, I'll get you to go through the applications again and sort them into age groups for me. Jeremy, I'll give you a quick look around the place, get you a key, and get you to take a look at the orientation package. And then we're going to jump in the council car, check out the buses and head out to our campsite.'

Tilly watched Jeremy as he absorbed what Bec was saying.

He nodded slowly. She couldn't help but think what a good-looking man he had become; he had been a handsome teenager, and she knew every inch of his face. It had been imprinted on her memory for ten years. He'd always worked out and kept himself in good shape, and it looked like he'd continued that. His hair was a bit short now, but Tilly's thoughts raced through her mind, and she pulled herself up short.

What the heck was she thinking? She had to remember what he had done to her, how he had really hurt her. It was all coming back to her now. Tilly clenched her hand, vowing to never forgive Jeremy Johnson as long as she lived.

No matter what her heart told her.

CHAPTER 21

Tilly

Bec sat in the front of the four-wheel drive with Jeremy at the wheel, while Tilly and Alice sat in the back. Tilly stared out the window at the passing landscape, trying not to look at the curls that brushed Jeremy's collar.

So far, they had maintained a friendly tone with each other. They had avoided personal topics and kept their relationship professional throughout the morning. When Bec asked if everyone was happy to visit the campsite after their morning tea break, they agreed to all travel out in the council's four-wheel drive.

Bec turned to Jeremy and asked, 'Did you finish filling out all those forms for driving? And did you leave a copy of your license with the shire office?'

Jeremy nodded. 'Yes, everything is in order.

But if anyone else wants to drive, don't feel like we have to stick with me.'

'You can drive, and we can chat,' Bec said.

'Okay,' Jeremy replied with a laugh.

Alice was quiet with Tilly in the back as they headed northwest. They were on the road to the Calthorpe's property, but they would turn off about five kilometres before the gate and go around the lake to the other side.

Apparently, the New Life company had built several new buildings there, including a camp kitchen, and a couple of breakout rooms, as well as the two bunkhouses. Tilly imagined it would be a lot fancier than the tents they'd camped in during the Year 12 retreat.

As Jeremy accelerated along the road, Alice turned to Tilly. 'I'm not being rude, but I'm just going to rest for a bit. I'm still not fully awake. The antihistamines I took to stop my nose from running always make me sleepy.'

'No problem at all,' Tilly replied. 'I'm happy to enjoy the scenery.'

The scenery that was so familiar to her. All she could think of was the time she had spent out here with Jeremy at the Year 12 retreat.

When they had still been a couple and making their plans for the future.

She wondered if he was thinking about it too. He'd been quite aloof since he had discovered they would be working together. She wondered if he was going to find it as hard as she was already.

Tilly knew she had to put the past behind her.

In the front, Bec and Jeremy were talking occasionally, but the sound of the wheels on the road drowned out most of their conversation. Tilly leaned back, closed her eyes, and tried not to dwell too much on the situation.

She knew she had to maintain professionalism and treat both Jeremy and herself as fellow coworkers. They were different people now than when they were teenagers, and she needed to focus on that. Jeremy was simply the other new youth worker at the centre, and she would deal with it.

After another fifteen minutes of driving, they arrived at their destination. Alice still wasn't looking well, and Bec suggested that she shouldn't have come.

'I wanted to see what Chloe and Rosie have done out here,' she insisted, her voice thick. 'I think it's the tablets rather than the cold making Alice sound like that,' Tilly reassured Bec.

'As long as you're better by Easter. It will be all hands on deck that long weekend,' Bec said.

As they drove closer to the lake, Tilly's memories flooded back. The road was familiar, and they passed a couple of old sheds and a windmill that she remembered from the bus trip out here in Year 12.

An unbidden smile tilted her lips; they had been happy days, and in a way, she was pleased she was back here.

She and Jeremy would just have to make their peace.

CHAPTER 22

Ten years ago

Their school classroom was set up with rows of desks, but tonight, in recognition of the camp's bonding goal, the Year 12 students sat in chairs placed in a half circle. It was the last night of the senior school retreat, and the group of Year 12 students was gathered to learn some valuable study tips before heading into their final exams. It was probably going to be the last time many of them would be together.

Mr Thompson stood in the middle of the circle in front of the data projector, which was connected by two extension cords along the grass to the single power point in the old camp kitchen. The light illuminated his face, displaying a slide titled "Top 5 Things You Need to Know About Successful Study."

'Rightio, everyone.' Tilly nudged Jeremy as

Mr Thompson began. Unbeknownst to the elderly teacher who was teaching his last class before retirement, the students called him Mr Rightio because he began every sentence with that word. 'Let's go through these tips. I promise they're worth your attention.'

Tilly and Jeremy sat next to each other, Tilly's iPad in her lap, Jeremy's pen tapping absently on the side of his chair.

'First.' Mr Thompson pointed to the slide that was displayed on the side of a tent. 'Plan your study time. Make a timetable and stick to it. Scheduling is the key.'

Jeremy leaned closer to Tilly, whispering with a grin. 'Rightio, Tils. How's your timetable looking?'

'I'm working too many hours at the store.' She smiled, her cheeks flushing a little. 'I might need some help with that.'

Mr. Thompson continued. 'Second, find

your study style. Some people are visual learners, others are auditory. Figure out what works best for you.'

Tilly typed a note, and Jeremy scribbled a quick diagram of different learning styles. They exchanged looks, knowing they had very different approaches to studying.

'Third, take regular breaks. Your brain needs time to process information. Don't cram the night before!'

Tilly nudged Jeremy playfully. 'Hear that? No more last-minute all-nighters for you.'

Jeremy grinned, shaking his head. 'I'll try, but no promises.'

'Fourth,' Mr. Thompson said, 'Practise past papers. You can get them on CDs from the school library.'

'And on the education website,' Tilly whispered. 'He's so old-fashioned.'

Mr Thompson looked over the top of his

glasses at her.

'Sorry,' she mouthed.

'They're the best way to get used to the exam format and timing. Multiple-choice questions first, then the short answer ones, and then the essays. Work out how much time you need for each, and stick to it when you practise.'

Both Tilly and Jeremy nodded, making more notes. They'd heard this tip before, but Mr. Thompson's emphasis made it seem more urgent.

'And finally,' Mr Thompson concluded, 'look after yourselves. Eat well, sleep well, and get some exercise. No late nights.' He tapped the side of his nose. 'And no end-of-year parties until after the exams. A healthy body means a healthy mind.'

The session wrapped up, and the students dispersed for dinner. After the meal, Jeremy was on scullery duty with the other male students, and Tilly wandered down to the water's edge.

She knew he would follow her when the camp kitchen was clean.

When he appeared beside her, he held out his hand, and she laced her fingers through his.

'Soft hands,' she giggled.

'Dishpan hands,' he retorted. 'I had to scour the pot the spag bol was cooked in. I vote we get a dishwasher when we set up our flat in Brisbane.'

'Waste of money,' she replied.

Tilly looked away over the water. Jeremy's family was well off. His dad was a hard businessman, owning three shops in town. Her dad was a farmhand, and they rented in Augathella. She knew that Mr Johnson didn't like her, and she always felt uncomfortable when she was alone at the store with him. She knew that he looked down his nose at her family.

Tilly and Jeremy walked hand-in-hand towards the lake. A fat yellow moon was rising, casting a shimmering path on the water.

'It's beautiful,' Tilly said, looking at the moonlit lake.

'Yeah,' Jeremy agreed, his voice soft. 'Really beautiful.'

They walked in silence for a while, the sounds of the camp fading into the background. When they reached a secluded spot by the water and stood in the dappled shadows of a huge tree, Jeremy turned to Tilly.

'I'm really glad we came to this camp,' he said. 'It's been . . . nice, spending time together. Better than being at school. Or seeing you when you finish at our shop.'

Tilly nodded, her heart beating faster. 'Yeah, me too. It feels like old times. Before, we were worrying about our final exams.'

Jeremy looked at her, his eyes reflecting the moonlight. 'I love you, Tils.'

Before Tilly could respond, Jeremy gently

cupped her face with both hands. They stood there, the lapping small waves from the gentle breeze, the only sound breaking the silence. Slowly, Jeremy leaned in, and Tilly met him halfway. Their lips touched in a soft, lingering kiss, a gentle promise of what was ahead.

When they finally pulled apart, Tilly smiled up at him as he held her hands in his. 'That was pretty special.'

Jeremy grinned, his thumb brushing against her palm. 'I can't wait until we've moved to Brisbane together.'

They stood there a little longer, the full moon watching over them, their futures stretching out before them like the shimmering path on the water.

CHAPTER 23

Tilly – Choice for Youth office

Three weeks later

'Tilly, are you still good with spreadsheets?'

Jeremy stood by her desk. She looked up, managing to keep her heart rate at a normal pace. Being in the office with him and working with him had become easier over the past three weeks, and they had slipped into an almost easy collegial relationship. There was no personal conversation and no socialising, but when they were in the office, it was as though he was simply someone she worked with. She managed not to think about her feelings; she learned to switch them off when she left the flat each morning, but she suffered for doing that as Jeremy filled her thoughts and dreams as soon as she got home each night.

She'd finally got over the shock she'd had

when she'd discovered that Jeremy had moved into the same block of flats as she had.

At least he wasn't next door; he was at one end, and Tilly was at the other. But it made it hard because sometimes from her window, she'd see him going out to the bin, the mailbox, or backing his car from the carport. It was as though he was with her twenty-four hours a day. She knew when he was home, and she wondered where he was when he went out and listened for him to come home. It was doing her head in.

At the end of the second week in the office, Tilly drove up to Augathella to help Nana move and had some respite from her thoughts of Jeremy. Nana had been happy, and they'd shared some laughs as they'd ferried some of her belongings to the aged care facility.

Tilly snapped back to the present, aware that Jeremy was waiting for her answer. She looked up at him before quickly looking away. He was staring at her, and his expression was strange.

Almost yearning.

'Yes, what do you need?' she asked briskly, opening Excel on her computer.

'I'm having problems with the formula for the budget graph.'

'Okay, let me show you.' She quickly demonstrated the steps. He nodded and went back to his desk.

For the rest of the afternoon, Tilly couldn't forget the way Jeremy had looked at her. He'd looked miserable but hopeful. Maybe he was finding it hard working in the same office too.

Alice was Bec's second-in-charge and mostly stayed in the office. Bec rostered Jeremy and Tilly together to go out to the various homes, where they checked on some of their clientele. Anything related to the centre and the camp organisation meant they were in the council four-wheel drive together.

In one way, it was good. It made working with Jeremy so much easier because they were used to spending time together again, as *colleagues,* not as ex-friends and certainly not as lovers.

Luckily, they hadn't had to go back out to the lake together.

Yet.

Memories of that night by the lake ten years ago wouldn't leave Tilly, and in a way, she was dreading being out there over Easter, which was now only a week away.

She jumped when the door slammed loudly.

Bec strode into the office, a thunderous look on her face. 'Alice, Jeremy, Tilly, drop whatever you're working on. We need to talk now. In the meeting room. Please.'

Alice caught Tilly's eye as she left her desk. Tilly raised her eyebrows and shook her head as she followed Alice and Jeremy into the meeting room.

'What's wrong, Bec?' Jeremy sat with his hands folded on the table in front of him, and Tilly looked away.

Stop looking at him, she told herself sternly.

'One of our councillors has read an article in the media about a camp in Western Australia being fined $100,000 because a couple of kids ran away from the camp one night,' Bec explained.

Jeremy and Tilly looked at each other, and Tilly could swear she saw a small smile form on his lips.

'So, how does that impact our camp?' Alice asked.

'Well, Mrs Cahill has asked that it be cancelled until she can find out more information. She's raising it at the council meeting tonight.'

Tilly shook her head. 'Why? We've had all

this wonderful stuff donated for the camp. I mean, the buildings and everything, and we're not paying for them. She should be grateful for the opportunities being provided for us.'

'What can we do?' Jeremy asked.

'Three things,' Bec said. 'Alice, I want you to go through all of our documentation, all of our risk assessments. All of the kids' applications. Check that all their medical stuff is definitely listed. Check if we've missed anything there in terms of medication. You know the drill.'

Alice nodded. 'Okay, what else?'

'That's all for you. I'm going to meet with Mrs Cahill and see if I can talk some sense into her before the meeting. She's talking about going to the media. The mayor is just rolling his eyes. He's supportive of all our initiatives, but she likes to cause difficulty.'

'Jeremy and Tilly, I want you to drive out to the campsite. I've called the builders and the

New Life team. They'll meet you there. Go over anything that you think needs more explanation, and check that we've got all of the warranty documents, hot water systems, cooktops, heaters, and anything else you can think of. This is absolutely doing my head in,' Bec said, slumping back in her chair

'There'll be so many disappointed kids if the camp doesn't go ahead,' Jeremy said. 'The kids have all been buzzing about it.'

'You've got it there, Jeremy. They are. Let's look on the positive side.' Bec sighed. 'We've crossed all our Ts and dotted our Is. If you guys can just do that for me— what time is it now?' Bec glanced down at her watch. 'It's almost noon now. By the time you get out there, have your meeting, and get back, it'll probably be about four hours. Alice, anything that's missing, chase up. I'll go and see Mrs Cahill now. Let's plan on meeting back here at four o'clock. We'll bring all of our documentation back together, make sure it's all fine. I'll get it all sorted, and I'll go to the council meeting. I'm sure she's going to raise it. If we're prepared, we'll be right, and the rest of the council should be fine, but we just can't afford to leave any stone unturned.' Bec grabbed the keys and was out the door before they could blink.

'Right, I'll get the paper trail in place. I'll see you at four,' Alice said, heading to her computer.

'You ready to go now, Tilly?' Jeremy looked at her.

'Yes, I'll grab my lunch out of the fridge. I'm starving. I was just about to go and get it when Bec arrived.'

Tilly nodded to herself. *Look what normal conversations we can have.*

'Yeah, I'm hungry too. I was going to go down to the bakery, but I won't have time now.'

Tilly stared at him and then dropped her eyes as Jeremy held hers. 'I've got two sandwiches. I'm happy to share.'

'Thank you. And I've got a couple of apples. I'll throw them in. We'll have a picnic in the car on the way out.'

Tilly nodded and disappeared into the kitchen. Well, she'd known she was going to have to face being out at the lake with Jeremy eventually. She was better off getting it over and done with before camp started.

Their conversation was light as they shared their food in the car as Jeremy drove out to the lake. Passing him a sandwich and then one of his apples as he drove brought back old times when they would go driving in his old Land Rover ute on weekends.

Not only was the builder onsite when Jeremy parked outside the bunkhouse, but two other cars were parked beside him. Chloe and Rosie, and their husbands were talking to Rod, the builder, on the veranda of the cookhouse. Chloe turned around and smiled at them. 'Hi guys, a bit of a hiccup, I hear.'

'But I'm sure we'll get it sorted,' Rosie chimed in.

'I hope so. There will be a lot of disappointed kids if we don't,' Tilly replied as they walked up the steps.

'It's really sad that one person can be like that,' Rosie said.

'It is,' Chloe said, 'but she obviously has other problems that make her unhappy, and this makes her feel good about herself. She's making sure everything is right for the kids.'

Rosie shook her head. 'You're a good person, Chloe. Kinder than I am.'

It took a couple of hours to go through all of the documentation with Rod. He showed them how to switch off the hot water system and demonstrated the fire extinguisher, although they all knew how to use it. They decided to do it anyway.

'We were all going to come out the night before the camp started,' Chloe said. 'Is that okay with you?'

Jeremy nodded. 'I'm sure it'll be okay with Bec. After all, it's your land and buildings. You don't have to ask our permission.'

'No, it's a community facility,' Chloe said.

'Okay, I think we've got everything. Do you guys have all the paperwork from Rod?'

This time Tilly nodded. 'We do. So, we'll see you soon. I guess you're going to the council meeting tonight to support Bec. We'll all be there.'

'Rosie and I will be. The guys have to go back to take over at the store. We're opening for late-night shopping tonight. A trial run.'

Tilly grinned. 'You guys are amazing, not

only a department store in Augathella but late-night shopping too!'

The three vehicles left. Jeremy and Tilly stood as they drove out. All of a sudden, it seemed very quiet with just the two of them. A crow cawed in the tree above them, and Tilly jumped.

'I think there's one thing that we need to do,' Jeremy said. 'I'm happy to go and do it unless you want to come for a walk with me.'

'What's that?' Tilly asked. His eyes were still on her, and she looked up at the crow.

'Considering the nature of Mrs Cahill's concern, I think we need to have photographic evidence for the council tonight, seeing her biggest worry is that the kids are going to wander off. I thought I'd go down with my phone and take photos of the fences that are on either edge of the camp, the gates, and how I've got padlocks on them, and also that we've got some kayaks and life buoys down on the edge of the lake. That way, she can't talk about kids disappearing down by the lake.'

Tilly bit her lip. 'We probably also need to make up a roster for the camp. I know we've got rosters for supervision, but it ends at lights out. And we need to—'

She stumbled over her words as she remembered why she'd thought of this and then took a deep breath. 'I think we need to have a roster for after the kids have all gone to bed because we do have some 16 and 17-year-olds here. I think someone needs to be stationed down by the lake at night.'

Jeremy's eyes met hers, and held. They both knew exactly what she was talking about. That night, down by the lake, which had started with a lingering kiss and more planning about moving to Brisbane, had ended up with a lot more; they knew firsthand what teenagers could get up to at the lake.

Jeremy grinned at her. 'More than most, perhaps?'

Suddenly, a load lifted off Tilly's shoulders. They were on the same wavelength. She understood Jeremy, and she knew exactly what he was saying.

She always had.

Tilly began to think about her opinion of Jeremy. No matter that she had had issues with his parents, the Jeremy she'd known then, and the Jeremy he had grown into as an adult, had been and was still a good person.

He wouldn't have abandoned her.

If she'd stayed in town longer, he would have come to see her, so Tilly knew she had to take some of the blame.

'Jeremy, I'll come down to the lake with you, but I also want to talk to you.'

'Talk to me?' he asked.

She nodded and kept her eyes on his. 'Yes, we really need to talk.'

She smiled as relief softened his features.

'I like the sound of that. We do need to talk, Tilly.'

CHAPTER 24

It seemed fitting to Tilly that she and Jeremy were going to try to resolve their issues by the lake; the lake where they had made their future plans and shared a night of passion together.

This time, as they walked through the trees to the water, they weren't hand-in-hand, but Jeremy kept glancing over at her and Tilly could see the happy anticipation on his face.

She felt a lot lighter too. Hopefully, once they talked it out, their time working together would be a lot easier.

She thought as they approached the last stand of trees leading to the lake's shore, that perhaps they could even be friends.

Six barbecue tables with bench seats had been placed along the lawn at the edge of the water.

Since their last visit here with Bec, gardens had been built, some with rock edges and some with timber benches in a square around the edges of the plants.

'I can't believe Chloe and Rosie and their group did this. It looks like these gardens have been here for years,' she said. A fully established tree was in the centre of each garden.

'They are amazing, and they do so much for the community. That's why we really have to have this first camp. I heard Bec mention the other day that there is a surprise ceremony with the mayor presenting them with a certificate on the first night.

They sat at a table closest to the water, opposite each other, and Jeremy placed his hands on the table in front of them. This time, Tilly looked at them without feeling self-conscious.

'What did you want to talk about, Tils? Us?'

She nodded. 'Our new relationship.'

'New?'

'As work colleagues. I'd like . . . I was hoping we could be friends too.'

Jeremy shook his head and looked away, and Tilly's heart fell. When he turned back, his eyes were intense.

'I can't be just a friend to you. That's not enough for me.' His voice shook. 'I still love you, Tilly. I've never stopped loving you.'

She went to speak, but he put his hand up. 'Let me finish.'

When Jeremy reached over and took her hand, she didn't pull away.

'I've never forgiven myself for not coming to see you that night. My father forbade me to leave the house, and I listened to him. I tried to text you, but there was no answer. By the time I got to your house the next morning, you had gone. Your parents wouldn't tell me where you were; even your mother would barely speak to me. They obviously thought I was like my father.'

'It's okay, Jeremy.' Tilly was still trying to process what he'd said about loving her. A kernel of warmth had formed in her chest and was slowly spreading through her whole body. 'I was young and impulsive, and I was so embarrassed. I thought somehow I'd brought it on myself.'

'What? The accusation of being a thief?'

'No, the other, and retaliating.'

Jeremy frowned and stared at her, and she *knew*.

'Retaliating to what?' he asked.

She took her hand away from his and waved it in a dismissive gesture. 'It doesn't matter. You don't need to know.'

'I do. What you need to know is that I have been looking for you for so long. I couldn't find you on social media; your parents moved away, and no one would tell me where you'd gone.

What you need to know is that I didn't speak to my father again before he died.'

'Oh, Jeremy, that is so sad.'

'No, he was a hard man. I've often thought of changing my name.'

'Changing your name?' Tilly frowned. 'Why?'

'I found out that weekend that I was adopted. I'd never known. That made it so much easier for me to leave. I'd never got on with him. He was a cruel and hard man. So I want you to tell me *exactly* what happened.'

'He assaulted me. He squeezed my breast, and he hurt me.'

Jeremy's face was white. 'The bastard.'

'I hurt him back,' Tilly admitted. 'I kneed him in the "you know whats". And then I fled and the next I heard he rang up and told Mum and Dad that I stole from the store. I've always thought you believed that I did.'

Tilly stood and walked around to the other side of the table. She placed her hands gently on Jeremy's shoulders. 'Did you really mean what you said about not being friends?'

'Telling you that I love you?' He stood, and his arms went around her. 'I did, and the way that you're looking at me gives me hope that you still love me. Even though it's been ten years? Ten long and lonely years.'

'You are my soulmate, Jeremy. You always have been, and yes, I do love you.'

Jeremy's head lowered, and they shared a brief but sweet kiss before he pulled back. 'As much as I hate to say it, we have to go. Bec and Alice will be waiting for us.'

EPILOGUE

With everyone's support, Bec was victorious, and the Easter camp went ahead. On Saturday night, the mayor presented the new Augathella residents with certificates of appreciation at a function. Half the town came to the night by the lake, and with their usual generosity, Chloe and her friends put on a free barbeque for about two hundred people. Even Councillor Cahill attended and was seen to smile.

Everyone was there. Matt Randall and Ben Riley were on the temporary stage singing to the crowd.

The three Cartwright boys whooped around because they had each won their age group in the Billy Cart Derby that morning. Their half-siblings, Megan and Munro, sat in their prams and whooped as loudly.

Callie put a hand to her head. 'I can't believe that pair can yell as loud as their brothers.'

'And Meggie is the loudest,' Braden said with a laugh as he put his arms around Callie.

Fallon Ingram grinned at Callie. 'So the family is complete?'

Callie looked up at Braden, and they shared a secret smile.

'What about you two?' she asked Fallon.

Fallon put one hand on her stomach. 'I think Augathella is going to need a larger school.'

Jenny Riley was there with Tom, all smiles as they chatted to their friends, and shared their good news. Tom had been diagnosed with an illness that presented the same symptoms as dementia, and the treatment had worked.

Kimberley and Quinn Calthorpe's news of a baby on the way had been met with great joy.

'We're due on the same date,' Sophie Mason

announced.

No one noticed, but Laura and Dr Harry shared a quiet smile. Their news would be around soon enough.

Gladys Tingle stole the show when she marched up to Jeremy and put her arms around him. 'About time, boy. Welcome to the family.'

The biggest announcement that night was when the mayor announced the date for the Spring Masquerade Ball.

After the town residents had left, Alice, Bec, and two volunteers went to the water to check for anyone who may have left the bunkhouses.

Jeremy smiled at Tilly, tugged her hand, and led her in the opposite direction to the dark side of the lake—the side where they had been before, ten years ago.

Tilly turned to him with a smile, and Jeremy pulled her into his arms, fitting together as if they had never been apart. He kissed her—a tender, lingering kiss that spoke of all the years lost and their future together.

THE END

Stay posted for **An Augathella Masquerade Ball,** where we leave Augathella in the last book of the Augathella Short and Sweet series.

Pre-orders available for: An Augathella Masquerade Ball

eBook:

https://books2read.com/u/4XNae5

Print:

https://annieseatonstore.ecwid.com/An-Augathella-Masquerade-Ball-Pre-order-September-2024-p660129078

OTHER PRINT BOOKS FROM ANNIE

Available on Annie's store and Amazon:

https://annieseatonstore.ecwid.com/

New Series: The Daughters of The Darling

1: From Across the Sea

2. Over the River (November 2024)

Other books

Whitsunday Dawn

Undara

Osprey Reef

East of Alice

Porter Sisters Series

Kakadu Sunset

Daintree

Diamond Sky

Hidden Valley

Larapinta

Kakadu Dawn

Pentecost Island Series

Pippa

Eliza

Nell

Tamsin

Evie

Cherry

Odessa

Sienna

Tess

Isla

Also available in three boxed sets

Books 1-3

Books 4-6

Books 7-10

The Augathella Girls Series

Outback Roads

Outback Sky

Outback Escape

Outback Wind

Outback Dawn

Outback Moonlight

Outback Dust

Outback Hope

Augathella Short and Sweet Series

An Augathella Surprise

An Augathella Baby

An Augathella Spring

An Augathella Christmas

An Augathella Wedding

An Augathella Easter

An Augathella Masquerade Ball

Sunshine Coast Series

Waiting for Ana

The Trouble with Jack

Healing His Heart

Sunshine Coast Boxed Set

The Richards Brothers Series

The Trouble with Paradise

Marry in Haste

Outback Sunrise

Richards Brothers Boxed Set

Bondi Beach Love Series

Beach House

Beach Music

Beach Walk

Beach Dreams

The House on the Hill

Second Chance Bay Series

Her Outback Playboy

Her Outback Protector

Her Outback Haven

Her Outback Paradise

The McDougalls of Second Chance Bay Boxed

Set

Love Across Time Series

Come Back to Me

Follow Me

Finding Home

The Threads that Bind

Love Across Time 1-4 Boxed Set

Bindarra Creek

Worth the Wait

Full Circle

Secrets of River Cottage

A Clever Christmas

A Bindarra Creek Duo

A Place to Belong

Four Seasons Short and Sweet

Ten Days in Paradise

Follow the Sun

Others

Deadly Secrets

Adventures in Time

Silver Valley Witch

The Emerald Necklace

Christmas with the Boss

Her Christmas Star

An Aussie Christmas Duo (the two Christmas novellas)

ABOUT THE AUTHOR

Annie lives in Australia, on the beautiful north coast of New South Wales. She sits in her writing chair and looks out over the tranquil Pacific Ocean.

She writes contemporary romance and loves telling stories that always have a happily ever after. She lives with her very own hero of many years and they share their home with Toby, the naughtiest dog in the universe, and Barney, the ragdoll puss, who hides when the four grandchildren come to visit.

Stay up to date with her latest releases at her website: http://www.annieseaton.net

AWARDS

2023: Winner of the long contemporary RUBY award for Larapinta

Finalist for the NZ KORU Award 2018 and 2020.

Winner ...Best Established Author of the Year 2017 AUSROM

Longlisted for the Sisters in Crime Davitt Awards 2016, 2017, 2018, 2019

Finalist in Book of the Year, Long Romance, RWA Ruby Awards 2016 Kakadu Sunset

Winner ...Best Established Author of the Year 2015 AUSROM

Winner ...Author of the Year 2014 AUSROM

Best Established Author, Ausrom Readers' Choice   2017

Book of the Year

www.ingramcontent.com/pod-product-compliance
Lightning Source LLC
Chambersburg PA
CBHW011222190726
48287CB00008B/2713